# JOURNEY THROUGH Ballidrempt

## DEREK FARMER

First published in Great Britain in 1995.
Text copyright © 1995 Derek Farmer.
The moral right of the author has been asserted.

Bloomsbury Publishing PLC, 2 Soho Square, London W1V 6HB.
A CIP catalogue record for this book is available from The British Library
ISBN 0 7475 2077 1
Text design by AB3.
Printed by Cox and Wyman Ltd, Reading, Berkshire.

# Chapter 1

—

Before the Journey nobody had even heard of the Land of Badlidrempt. It was just another place that didn't exist. Except that it did. It was there all the time. Waiting to be discovered. By a brother and sister. A boy inventor. And a woolly sausage. This is their story. You'll never believe it.

The brother and sister were Billy and Sandy Patrickson. The boy inventor was Peregrine Norbertson Smythe. Better known to his friends – and some of his enemies – as Brains. And the woolly sausage? Well, that was Brains's dog Grenville.

Grenville wasn't a sausage. He wasn't even a sausage dog. And he had less wool than a bald sheep. So why call him a woolly sausage? That comes later. What comes now is this –

Sandy, Billy, Brains and Grenville were in the shed at the bottom of Brains's garden.

'It's a robot.' That was Sandy.

'Wrong,' said Brains.

'A flying hatstand.' That was Billy.

'Wrong again.'

'Then what is it?'

Sandy and Billy were looking at Brains's latest invention. They were trying to guess what it was.

'What is it?' Brains repeated. He took off his glasses and cleaned them with an oily rag. 'I would have thought everybody could see that. Even Grenville.'

Sandy and Billy looked hopefully at Grenville. He had no idea what it was either. He shook his head. He shook it so hard that one of his ears turned inside out. Billy flipped it back into place with the toe of his shoe.

'I suppose I'd better tell you then?' Sometimes Brains was a real smuggins!

'No,' said Sandy. 'We don't give up that easy do we, Billy?'

'Yes,' said Billy. He was too hungry to play guessing games. He hadn't eaten since breakfast and it was almost ten o'clock.

'Oh no, we don't,' Sandy snapped.

She stared hard at the invention. What on earth was it?

Brains threw down the oily rag and put his glasses back on. He couldn't see a thing. They were dirtier than ever. He took them off and cleaned them with Grenville's tail.

'Hurry up,' he said. 'I've not got all day.'

Hunger was making Billy think better. 'I know what it is,' he called out. 'It's a hair cutting machine. You sit on the seat. The whatsit comes up. Swings round the thingamajig. And chops your hair off.'

Sandy pulled a face. 'Don't be stupid. There's no scissors. How can it cut hair?'

For a moment Billy was stumped. Then he had a brainwave.

'In that case,' he said. 'It's a hair cutting machine for bald men. They don't need scissors.'

'They don't need haircuts!'

'Need polishing though, don't they? It's a machine for polishing bald heads!'

Brains looked at Billy as though he'd gone crazy. 'I don't know who's more stupid. You or Grenville.'

Grenville poked his nose out from under the workbench. He knew who was more stupid.

Billy was. Grenville barked twice. A spanner dropped on his head. It bounced to the floor. The spanner, not Grenville's head. Grenville howled.

'Dopey dog!' said Billy. 'He needs his head examining.'

'So would you if you'd just had a spanner drop on it,' said Sandy.

Brains had one or two final adjustments to make. He gave a jolt to a bolt. Took a flail at a nail. And gave a twing to a spring. Then he stepped back to admire his invention.

Grenville crossed his eyes and rocketed into the air. Brains was standing on his tail.

'Sorry, Grenville,' said Brains. 'I thought it was Billy's foot.' He looked at Sandy and Billy. 'Any ideas?'

Sandy and Billy looked at the invention. Then they looked at each other. They still didn't have a clue what it was.

Brains had had enough. 'It's a bicycle!' he yelled.

'A bicycle?' said Sandy, scratching her head.

'That's nothing like a bicycle!' said Billy, scratching Grenville's head. 'You wouldn't even get down the garden path on that.'

'Well, that's where you're wrong.' Brains gave

one last whack to a tack. 'And I'll tell you something else. This is no ordinary bike. This is special.'

'What do you mean "special"?' Sandy asked.

'It falls to bits when you sit on it!' laughed Billy.

Grenville gave a low threatening growl.

'Shut up, Billy, you're upsetting Grenville,' Sandy snapped. 'How is it special, Brains?'

Brains put on his bike clips. 'You'll see,' he smirked. 'Time I tried it out.'

And with that Brains opened the door and wheeled the mysterious bicycle outside.

A couple of minutes later, Brains was sitting on the bike at the end of the garden. He was raring to go. But go where?

'Wouldn't you like to know!' said Brains mysteriously.

'Up the garden path,' said Sandy.

'I think that's where he's leading us,' Billy muttered.

Brains started pedalling. It was hard work but slowly the machine began to move. Up and down at first. Then side to side. Then round and about. In fact, it moved in every direction but forward.

Brains was puffing, panting, wheezing and gasping. The bike was clanking, clonking, squeaking and whirring. But still it refused to move forward.

Sandy and Billy watched in amazement as Brains's face turned the colour of a sunburnt beetroot.

'It's starting to work,' Brains croaked.

Billy couldn't control himself any longer. He began to laugh. A chuckle at first. Growing to a giggle. Then a guffaw. And finally a shoulder-shaking belly laugh.

'Billy!' Sandy warned. But she had to admit, Brains did look funny.

By now Billy was rolling on the ground clutching his sides.

Sandy tried to keep a straight face. But Billy's laugh could make a statue snigger. Sandy giggled. She gurgled and chortled. And before she knew it she was rolling on the ground next to Billy.

'I've never seen anything so funny,' Billy cackled. ' He's going up and down like a frog on a trampoline.'

Brains was not amused. Neither was Grenville. He grabbed hold of Billy's foot and tugged. Billy's shoe came off in his mouth and

Grenville shot backwards into the fish pond.

Billy and Sandy laughed louder than ever.

'You won't be laughing in a minute,' Brains gasped.

And Brains was right. Finally, the bike began to move forward. Brains pushed a lever. A deep rumble started. Gradually it got louder and higher. Building up to an ear-splitting whine.

Grenville howled. A spout of water shot from his mouth.

Sandy stopped laughing and sat up. She looked at Brains then rubbed her eyes. 'Billy!' she said. 'Something's happening. Brains is disappearing!'

Billy leapt to his feet. 'What do you mean disappearing?'

It was true. Both Brains and the bike were melting away. Vanishing into thin air. Already bits were going missing. In a moment they would be gone all together.

'Crikey!' Billy gulped. 'What do we do?'

'Grab him! Quick!' Sandy shouted.

Sandy, Billy and Grenville leapt forward. But it was too late. Their hands – and Grenville's teeth – grabbed thin air.

Both Brains and the bike had completely disappeared.

# Chapter 2

——

'This is mad!'

Sandy, Billy and Grenville were staring at the spot where Brains had been just a couple of seconds earlier.

'He can't really have disappeared,' Sandy said. 'It must be some sort of trick.'

'Yeah!' Billy agreed. 'A trick!'

It had to be a trick. Nobody could vanish into thin air. Not even Brains.

'He's hiding!' said Sandy. 'Waiting for us to go looking for him. Then he'll jump out to try and scare us.'

Grenville sniffed the air. What was that smell? It was a smell he knew well. He sniffed again.

'What's the matter with him?' asked Billy. 'Has he got a cold?'

'No, silly, he's searching for the scent,' said Sandy. 'Trying to get on the trail of Brains.'

Suddenly, Grenville thrust his nose down to the ground and shot off across the lawn.

'He's got the scent!' Sandy yelled. 'C'mon Billy, he's getting away.'

Sandy and Billy raced after Grenville – the Super Sniffer! It was like chasing a whirlwind.

Grenville's sensational sense of scent sent him whizzing down roads. Across fields. Through streams. Over bridges. In and out of ditches. Until at last his ceaseless searches ceased – back where they'd started in Brains's back garden!

Billy went bananas. 'You dopey dog!' he yelled.

'Billy!' Sandy hissed. 'No need to be nasty.'

'Well, he is a dopey dog,' Billy said. 'He's supposed to find Brains. He couldn't find a stink bomb in a perfume factory!'

But Grenville was still sniffing around. Suddenly he began scrabbling madly in the middle of the lawn.

Sandy and Billy watched in wonder as Grenville's claws ripped away at the ground. His legs were almost a blur as he dug deeper and deeper into the lawn. Stones, earth and clumps of turf flew through the air until at last Grenville howled in triumph.

'He's found something!' Sandy shouted. She grabbed hold of Grenville and heaved him to one side. What she saw at the bottom of the hole took her breath away. 'Oh, Billy!' she gasped. 'It's a skeleton!'

Sandy covered her face. Billy inched forward and peeped into the hole. 'It's not a skeleton,' he scoffed. 'It's just bones. Grenville must've buried them here years ago.'

Grenville grabbed the biggest, juiciest bone and disappeared under the privet hedge. Only his tail remained out in the open.

Billy picked up a bone and chucked it at the wagging tail. Grenville yelped and squirmed further under the hedge.

'Grenville!' Sandy snarled. 'You are a dopey dog. Brains disappears and all you can think about is food.'

'Food!' Billy licked his lips. 'That reminds me, I'm starving. I'm going home to get something to munch!'

Sandy grabbed Billy's shirt.

'You're going nowhere,' she told him angrily. 'We've got to find Brains. If this was a trick he would have turned up by now. I think he really did disappear.'

Billy shivered. This was getting spooky.

Perhaps Sandy was right. Perhaps Brains had disappeared. But how?

'It's that bike,' Sandy told him. 'He said it was special, didn't he?'

Billy's and Sandy's eyes met.

'The plans!' they said.

They raced for the shed. Brains always made notes and drew up plans before starting his inventions. If they could find the plans for the bike then they might be able to work out what had happened to him.

But where would the plans be?

They stood in the shed and looked around. It was hopeless. Brains was not only the brainiest person they knew, he was also the most untidy. The shed was cram-packed with bits and pieces. More pieces than bits actually. Some stacked on shelves. Some piled on benches. But most just in heaps on the floor.

'This could take for ever,' Billy groaned. 'The plans could be anywhere.'

'Then the sooner we start looking, the sooner we'll find them,' said Sandy.

Just then Grenville poked his nose around the shed door.

'And you can help as well, greedy guts,' Sandy shouted.

Grenville licked his lips and hiccupped. He was too full to argue.

Sandy, Billy and Grenville searched the shed from top to bottom but there was no sign of the plans for the bike. They had almost given up hope when –

Grenville sat on a nail!

It was a big sharp nail sticking up out of the floor. Not that Grenville sat on it for long. Within a couple of milliseconds he was rocketing towards the roof of the shed.

He landed with a bump and let out a howl that made the windows rattle.

'Oooooooooooogggghhhh!' howled Grenville.

'Dopey dog!' sniggered Billy. 'Fancy not seeing that.'

'He hasn't got eyes down there, Billy,' Sandy snapped. 'Now pull the nail out before it does some real damage.'

Grenville whimpered. It had already done some real damage! And he knew where.

Billy grabbed a pair of pliers and tugged at the nail. To everyone's surprise the floorboard swung up out of place.

'Look at this, sis!' said Billy. 'A secret hiding place under the floor!'

Billy shoved his hand down into the hole.

When he pulled it out again, he was clutching the plans.

For a moment, Grenville forgot his punctured parts and howled with excitement.

The plans were laid out on the floor of the shed. At the top was the heading 'PLAN FOR AN IDT BIKE'.

'IDT bike?' said Sandy. 'Wonder what that is?'

The answer was below. 'Using the Inter-Dimensional-Time bicycle – or IDT bike,' Brains had written, 'I will be able to travel through The Dimensions to visit new worlds where no human has ever been before.'

Sandy jumped to her feet. 'See? That's where Brains has disappeared to. He's gone to another world.'

Billy was horrified. 'He must be round the bend,' he said. 'Nobody with any sense would do that. There could be anything there.'

'Like what?' Sandy demanded.

Billy was shaking with fear. 'Like monsters!' he said. 'With long, dripping, yellow gnashers. And big, bulging, bloodshot eyes! And huge, bony hands just waiting to reach out and –'

A stomach-churning howl echoed round the shed. Grenville was not happy.

'It's all right, Grenville,' Sandy hugged

Grenville to her. 'Don't take any notice of Billy. He's just a wimp.'

'I am not,' Billy yelled. 'I'm just not going anywhere like that.'

'Yes you are,' said Sandy. 'Brains might be in danger. We've got to help him. He's our friend.'

Billy started to edge backwards. 'Not me!' he gulped. 'I've got better things to do than get eaten by monsters.' Billy made a dash for the door.

But he was too late. Grenville got there first.

Billy stared down at the quivering canine. 'It's no good looking at me like that,' he said. 'I'm not going.'

Grenville put his paws on Billy's shoulders and glared into his eyes. 'Grrrrrr!' he growled.

'Only joking, Grenville,' said Billy. He was having to think fast. 'I'd love to go off to another world to look for Brains. But how do we get there? Catch a bus!'

'We make another IDT bike,' said Sandy. 'Exactly like the the one Brains made. That'll get us there all right. Or are you too scared?'

'Me?' scoffed Billy. 'Scared? You must be joking. I'm not scared. I'm terrified.'

A slurpy wet tongue slurped Billy's face. It was Grenville's. Sandy was too busy building the bike.

\*   \*   \*

It was almost dark by the time Sandy put the finishing touches to IDT bike number two.

'There!' she said. 'Finished!'

'Looks a bit shaky to me,' said Billy. 'It'd fall apart if you gave it a good kick.'

'I won't be giving it a good kick.' She wheeled the bike into the garden. It was time to try it out.

Billy grabbed the handlebars. 'I'll steer,' he said.

'You won't,' said Sandy, pushing in front of him. 'That's my job. You get on the back.'

Grumbling to himself, Billy did as he was told. They were ready to go.

A slurpy, wet tongue licked Sandy's leg. It was Grenville's again. Billy was too busy trying not to fall off the back of the bike.

Sandy looked down. Grenville's tail began to wag hopefully. Sandy patted his head. 'Sorry, Grenville, you'll have to stay here.'

Grenville slumped to the floor and began to whimper.

'It's no good, Grenville,' said Billy. 'There's no room for you!'

The whimper turned to a whine.

'Look! Shut up! You're not coming and that's that.'

The whine turned to a howl. A heart-breaking howl which nobody could ignore. Billy pushed his fingers into his ears. 'Oh crikey!' he moaned. 'What a racket!'

'It's no good, Billy,' Sandy yelled over the howl. 'We'll have to take him.'

'How?' asked Billy. 'Whoever heard of a dog riding a bike! He'd drop off before we'd gone ten metres.'

'Not if we squeeze him in between us,' said Sandy.

That was all Grenville needed. As if by magic, the howling stopped and a large hairy dog scrambled up between Sandy and Billy.

'Woah!' he said finally, when he was firmly wedged in place.

'That means he's ready,' said Sandy.

'What do we do now?' asked Billy.

'Start pedalling,' Sandy told him.

They started to pedal. It was hard work. Every push on the pedal was an enormous effort. But as their legs built up speed, it got easier and easier. And the pedals started to whizz round faster and faster. Until at last the machine began to move. Up and down. Then side to side. Then round and about. And finally, when they had almost given up hope – forward.

Immediately, Sandy pushed the lever and the deep rumble they had heard earlier began. Slowly it built up, just as before, to an ear-splitting whine.

The bike started to shake. Sandy struggled to hold on to the handlebars but it was almost impossible. It was like trying to ride an earthquake.

There was no doubt about it. Something was happening. The world around them seemed to be shimmering. Going hazy at the edges. Dissolving away. Disappearing in front of their eyes.

The noise was deafening now and Sandy had to scream at the top of her voice to make herself heard. 'It's starting to work. We're on our way, Billy. Keep pedalling!'

But Billy had a problem. 'I can't, Sandy,' he shouted. 'I'm falling off the back. The bike's slipping away from under me.'

'Hold on, Billy!' Sandy screamed. 'You've got to hold on.'

But it was no good. Billy had completely lost his grip. 'I can't, sis,' he yelled. 'I'm being left behind. Sandy! I'm fallllllliiiinnnnggg!'

Desperately Sandy turned and grabbed for Billy. But it was too late. Billy had gone!

# Chapter 3

—

A split second later, the Inter-Dimensional-Time Bicycle crashed through a blanket of branches and landed in the middle of a forest clearing.

Sandy untangled herself from the battered bike and looked around. She was alone.

Where was Billy? If he'd fallen off on the journey through The Dimensions he could be anywhere. She might never see him again.

She closed her eyes and tried to think. The sound of Billy's voice was going round and round in her head. 'Sandy! I'm falliiiinnngg!' Then she remembered a second sound. A dog yelping in pain. Grenville! Where was he? Perhaps he'd fallen off too.

Somewhere a branch snapped like a bullet. Sandy held her breath. 'I am not scared. I am not scared,' she told herself.

But she was.

There was a rustle of leaves behind her. She twisted round. 'Billy!' she gasped. 'Is that you?'

There was a low moaning noise. Then one of the bushes spoke. 'Who else do you think it is? I'm over here. I fell in this bush as we landed. Get me out, will you?'

Sandy looked round. 'Which bush are you in?'

'This one.'

One of the bushes shook.

Sandy looked at it. It had thorns as long as her fingers. 'I'm not putting my hands in there,' she said. 'Just push your way out. It won't hurt if you do it quickly.'

'Says who?' said the voice in the bush.

'It's a well known fact.'

'Oh all right.' Billy didn't sound too sure. But a moment later there was a scream of agony and a badly punctured Billy burst out of the bush. He fell in a heap like a popped balloon.

'I thought you said it wouldn't hurt,' he moaned.

'It didn't,' grinned Sandy. 'I didn't feel a thing.'

She'd never been so pleased to see her brother. But she didn't want him to know that.

'I thought you'd fallen off and been left behind,' she told him.

Billy crossed his eyes and tried to squeeze a

thorn out from the end of his nose. 'I would have been, only I grabbed hold of something as I fell and that pulled me through.'

'What was it?'

'I dunno. But if I hadn't grabbed it I would have been a gonner.' Billy stopped suddenly in mid-squeeze. 'I just thought. Where's Grenville?'

Billy rolled over and sat on a pile of leaves. An instant later, the pile of leaves rolled over and sat on Billy.

'Ugghh!' said Billy.

'Ruff!' said the pile of leaves.

Nobody could mistake that sound.

'Grenville!' Sandy yelled as the pile of leaves erupted. 'Are you OK?'

Grenville started to whimper. Then he turned and gently licked his tail. Or at least, what was left of his tail. The end of it was completely bald!

'So that was what I grabbed hold of when I fell,' said Billy. He started to snigger. A dog with a bald tail was quite a sight.

Grenville's top lip began to curl. But Billy didn't take the warning.

'Never mind, Grenville, you can always get a tail wig,' he laughed.

He didn't laugh for long. It's hard to laugh when a dog is sitting on your head. Even when he has got a bald tail.

Sandy smiled. Things were back to normal again. 'Better say sorry,' she told Billy.

'All right, I'm sorry. Now let me get up.'

Grenville twisted round and licked Billy's face. He was forgiven. For now.

Billy dried his face and looked around.

'Wherever we are, I don't like it,' he hissed. 'It's spooky! Let's go home.'

'No,' said Sandy. 'We've come to find Brains. And we're not going home till we've found him. Now come on!'

But before they could come on, they were frozen to the spot by what sounded like a distant gunshot.

'Don't panic,' said Sandy. 'It's only a branch snapping.'

'Yes,' said Billy. 'And I'm a lemon meringue pie!'

Another gunshot rang out.

Six eyes blinked. Three throats gulped. Three mouths opened. And one tongue flopped out. It was Billy's.

More gunshots. Closer this time.

Grenville threw back his head and howled.

'Look, Grenville,' snapped Sandy, 'when we want somebody to do wolf impressions we know where to come. Until then shut up.'

A bullet whizzed through the clearing.

'They're coming this way,' gulped Billy.

Already, angry voices were shouting and bellowing as bodies crashed through the undergrowth towards the clearing.

Sandy took control. 'Quick! Into the thorn bushes.'

And into the thorn bushes they dived. After all, thorn holes were better than bullet holes.

Moments later, the clearing was filled with hordes of yelling, screaming bodies. Feet ran in every direction. Guns were fired. Confusion was everywhere. Then –

'Siiiiiilence!' a huge voice bellowed. And everything went quiet.

'That is better,' a second voice wheedled. 'There must be silence for the Great Grazzo. No person must be making the noises. Or they will be in the biggest of troubles. And –'

'Squirm!' the first voice interrupted.

'Yes, Grazzo?' said Squirm.

'Tighten the teeth.'

Squirm bowed his head. 'Oh yes, Grazzo,' he oozed. 'Soon no teeth will be tighter than –'

'Squirm!' Grazzo interrupted again.

'Yes, Grazzo?'

'Shut up.'

'Yes, Grazzo.'

'Now,' Grazzo turned to the Hordes. 'Listen to me. You are all blundering blubberheads!'

The Hordes began to babble and gabble. Those farthest away began to mutter and splutter. One or two even mumbled and grumbled.

'Silence!' Grazzo thundered. 'If I, the Great Grazzo, say you are blubberheads – blundering or unblundering – then you are blubberheads. And this is the reasons why. First, you let the wizard escape in a blizzard. Then you fail to follow his trail. And now, if you please, you get lost in the trees!'

'Oh Grazzo,' sighed Squirm. 'Such beautiful, beautiful poetry.'

Grazzo battered Squirm about the knees. 'Squirm, you germ, unless I have silence there will be violence.'

Squirm tightened his teeth and locked his lips.

Grazzo turned back to the Hordes. 'I, the Great Grazzo, is not the happy man. And when Grazzo is not happy, then no one must be happy.'

The Hordes shifted uneasily from foot to foot. Some, with three legs, shifted uneasily from foot to foot to foot.

Grazzo froze them with an icy glare. 'So I say to you just three words. Find the Wizard – now!'

'That is four words, Grazzo,' said Squirm. 'Find the Wizard now is four words.'

'Shut up, Squirm.'

'Yes, Grazzo.'

'The Wizard must be found. Ten bags of plastic bottle tops to the one who finds him.'

The Hordes began to buzz with excitement.

Squirm threw his cap in the air. 'Ten bags of plastic bottle tops!' he yelled. 'Such wonderful, wonderful treasures. Three boos for the most generous, Great Grazzo!'

Three hearty boos rang round the clearing. Grazzo grinned back at the Hordes. 'Too kind! Too kind!' he smirked. 'Now look and find.'

And as quickly as they'd come, they'd gone.

# Chapter 4

—

Sandy poked her head out from under the bush. The clearing was clear. 'It's OK,' she said. 'They've gone!'

One by one, they rolled out into the open.

'I don't like the sound of them one bit,' said Billy.

'Woah! Woah!' Grenville agreed. He didn't like the sound of them two bits!

Sandy shivered. 'They sounded pretty nasty, didn't they? Especially that one – what was his name?'

'Grrrr!' Grenville growled.

'Yes, that's right,' Sandy nodded. 'Grrrrr-azzo! What are they going to do to the Wizard if they find him?'

'Who cares?' said Billy. 'What would they do if they found us?'

'I don't want to find out,' said Sandy. 'Best get

away before they come back. Which way did they go?'

Billy stretched out his arm and spun round like a top. 'They went that way. That way. That way. That way. And that way!'

'All right,' said Sandy. 'Which way didn't they go?'

Billy pointed straight up in the air. 'They didn't go that way.'

Grenville barked and did his impression of an arrow – his nose pointing ahead, his tail straight out behind.

'See,' said Sandy. 'They didn't go that way, either. You're a genius, Grenville.' Sandy patted his head.

If Grenville had been a cat he would have purred with pleasure. But he wasn't so he just wagged his tail.

It didn't wag for long. There was a problem. There was no way out of the clearing.

A couple of minutes earlier there had been gaps everywhere. Places where Grazzo and the Hordes had run into and out of the clearing. But now the branches were all around again. Caging them in.

'There's something weird about this place,' Billy whispered. 'Let's go home now.'

'Not until we've found Brains,' Sandy told him.

'Ruff!' Grenville agreed.

'See?' said Sandy. 'Two against one. Now let's get out of here.'

'How?'

'We'll break a way through.'

Sandy reached out and snapped off a branch. Almost before she could take her hand away another one grew in its place.

Sandy looked at Billy.

Billy looked at Grenville.

Grenville looked puzzled.

Billy broke off a branch, then a twig, then a leaf. Each time a new one appeared.

'This is just not possible,' Billy insisted.

'Oh yes it is,' said a voice from behind.

Billy, Sandy and Grenville whirled round. There in the middle of the clearing stood a long, straggly figure with a long, straggly white beard.

'Where did you come from?' gasped Sandy.

'What does it matter?' said the mouth above the beard. 'What's important is where I'm going.'

'And where's that?' asked Billy.

'Away from Grazzo and Squirm. They're after me, you know.'

'You mean you're the Wizard they're all looking for?' said Sandy.

The stranger looked rather pleased with himself. 'Yes,' he admitted. 'Canticle's the name.'

'Canticle!' Billy sniggered. 'That's a funny name.'

'Not for a Wizard it isn't,' the Wizard snapped. 'Anyhow, I can't stand chatting to you. I've got to get away.'

Canticle hurried towards the edge of the clearing.

Billy folded his arms smugly. 'It's no good,' he said. 'You won't get through. We've already tried.'

'We'll see about that,' said the Wizard. He raised one arm. Then with a twirl of the fingers and a flick of the thumb he made a magic sign. Slowly the branches parted.

'There!' he said. 'Now if you want to get out of this forest alive, you'd better come with me. It's your only chance. And bring that woolly sausage with you.'

'That's not a woolly sausage,' said Sandy. 'That's Grenville.'

Grenville – the woolly sausage – growled.

Canticle shrugged his shoulders. 'I've not got time to argue.'

He clicked his fingers. A path through the undergrowth appeared.

'This way!' said Canticle.

And so the journey began.

Sandy, Billy, Grenville and the IDT bike followed the Wizard along the forest path. Sometimes in the distance they heard voices. Then Canticle stopped and snapped his fingers. Right away branches closed. Hiding them from view. Once the voices had gone away he clicked again and they were back on the path. Until finally the forest came to an end and the path became a rough cart track.

'Time for a rest,' said Canticle. 'We should be safe here for a while.' He sat down behind a hedge and took off his shoes.

A terrible smell wafted through the air. Billy and Sandy moved further away. Grenville covered his nose with his ears. And three birds in the hedge dropped off the perch.

'Something wrong?' said Canticle.

'What a stink!' Billy whispered.

'What was that?' the Wizard snapped.

'He said "Got to think!"' Sandy lied.

'Think what?'

Sandy thought fast. 'Think – why are you running away from Grazzo and Squirm? I mean, if you're really a Wizard why don't you just turn them into frogs or something?'

Canticle looked at them as though they were stupid. 'Because they've got my Magic Watch, of course,' he snarled.

'Magic Watch?' said Sandy. 'Don't you mean magic wand?'

'No!' Canticle snapped. 'I mean Magic Watch. It's more useful than a magic wand. Helps me do magic and tells me the time as well. Without it, I'm almost helpless. All I can do is a bit of light sorcery. Not nearly enough to overcome the pure evil of Grazzo and Squirm.'

'So how did they get your magic watch?' Billy asked.

'Sneaked up on me while I was asleep. Knocked me out and took it away. Then they put me in their Circus.'

'What Circus?'

'The Great Grazzo's Circus of the Wild, Weird and Wonderful.'

'Which were you supposed to be?' asked Billy. 'Wild, Weird or Wonderful?'

'Wonderful, of course.' Canticle glared at Billy as though he would have turned him into a three-legged frog if he'd had his Magic Watch with him. 'It's strange creatures like you and that Woolly Sausage he puts in the Weird part. So you'd better watch out!'

Billy swallowed hard and hid behind the Woolly Sausage. The Woolly Sausage covered his eyes with his ears and pretended he wasn't there.

'Anyway,' Canticle continued, 'that's where I was until last night. Then I escaped from my cage by tricking Squirm. I told him I'd lost my voice! And when he let me out to look for it, I ran off!'

All the time that he'd been speaking, Canticle had been rubbing the bottom of his feet.

'Are your feet very sore, Mr Canticle?' Sandy asked.

Canticle started to pull his shoes back on. 'Of course they are. So would yours be if you'd walked as far as I have.'

The Wizard stood up and took a few steps forward. Suddenly he stopped and pointed at the IDT bike.

'What's that?' he demanded.

'Just a bicycle,' said Sandy.

'An Inter-Dimensional-Time bicycle,' Billy chipped in.

Canticle was looking interested. 'What does it do?'

'You ride on it,' said Billy. 'That's how we got here.'

'Have you come far?' asked the Wizard, examining the handlebars.

'Miles and miles,' said Billy.

Canticle tried out the saddle. 'How are your feet?' he asked.

Billy was puzzled. It seemed like a strange question. 'Fine!' he said.

Canticle placed his feet on the pedals.

'How does it work?'

Billy told him.

The Wizard's eyes lit up. 'How clever! Who made it?'

'That's a long story,' said Sandy.

But she told it all the same.

'You haven't seen Brains, have you?' she asked when she'd finished.

Canticle shook his head. 'No. Grazzo's probably got him by now.'

'Grazzo!'

'His spies are everywhere. Nothing happens in the Land of Badlidrempt without him finding out.'

'The Land of Badlidrempt!' Sandy repeated. 'Is that where we are?'

'Yes. And it's full of the strangest, nastiest,

ugliest people you'll ever meet. Go home now while you still can. That's what I'm going to do.'

'I thought this was your home,' said Sandy.

Canticle shivered and poked his tongue out in disgust. 'This place? Home? No, I come from the Land of Sorcerers.'

'The Land of Sorcerers? Is that far?' asked Sandy.

'It is when you've got sore feet,' said Canticle. 'That's why I'm taking your machine.'

'What?' said Sandy.

'Yes,' smiled Canticle. 'I'll get to the Land of Sorcerers much more quickly on that.'

Billy grabbed the IDT bike. 'You're not taking this,' he yelled. 'We need it. To get back home.'

Canticle ran his long, straggly fingers through his long, straggly beard. 'Sorry,' he said. 'You can have it back when I've finished with it. If you can get to the Land of Sorcerers, of course.' Canticle raised one hand in the air. 'Nice meeting you,' he called. 'Sorry you've got to go!'

'We're not going anywhere,' said Sandy.

'Oh yes you are,' warbled the Wizard.

With a twirl of the fingers and a flick of the thumb, he made a magic sign.

The next thing they knew, Billy, Sandy and

Grenville were flying through the air. When they landed, both the Wizard and the IDT Bike were far, far away.

# Chapter 5

—

Billy, Sandy and Grenville sat in the dust at the side of the road and blinked.

'This is just a bad dream,' said Billy.

They blinked again.

It wasn't a bad dream. It was Badlidrempt. Badlidrempt was worse than a bad dream. It was still there when you woke up.

Grenville put his head between his paws and whimpered. Billy moaned.

'It's not as bad as it seems,' Sandy told them.

'No,' said Billy. 'It's worse.'

Billy was right. It was worse. Brains was still missing. And now Canticle had stolen the IDT bike. Without that, they were stuck. There was no way home.

'But once we find Brains we'll be all right,' said Sandy. 'He's got his IDT bike.'

'What if we don't find him?' said Billy. 'What if he's already gone home?'

'Brains wouldn't go home without us,' Sandy scoffed.

'He doesn't know we're here,' Billy pointed out.

But Sandy wasn't listening. She was looking along the road. In the distance was a bus stop.

'Come on,' said Sandy. 'There are people waiting. Perhaps they've seen Brains.'

There were two people waiting at the bus stop. One was Tib the other was Kal. Tib and Kal were identical friends. Identical friends are like identical twins but they're not related. They just grow to look like each other because they're always together.

Tib and Kal were tall and skinny with hair that looked like a mass of cobwebs. It looked like a mass of cobwebs because it was a mass of cobwebs. In fact, they were covered in cobwebs from head to foot.

They had their backs to Sandy, Billy and Grenville. But suddenly one of them turned round and said, 'About time too!' I think it was Tib.

'We've been waiting, you know,' said the other. Probably Kal.

'For us?' asked Sandy.

'For anything,' said Tib and Kal together. 'Why not join us?'

Billy grabbed hold of Sandy's arm.

'Don't go too close,' he whispered. 'They're seriously weird.'

Sandy took a step back. So did Billy. He fell over Grenville. Grenville yelped.

'Keep that thing away from us,' said Tib. If it was Tib.

'It's seriously weird,' said Kal. It must've been Kal.

'Been waiting long?' Sandy asked.

'All our lives,' said Tib. 'It's what we do. We're waiters.'

'Waiters?'

'Yes. We wait for things.'

'Wait for what?' Billy was back on his feet.

'Whatever turns up.'

'Everything turns up if you wait long enough,' said Kal. 'You're the third thing to turn up today.'

Billy turned to Sandy. 'Like I said – weird.'

'Row! Row!' Grenville agreed with knobs on.

But Sandy had had a thought. 'What else has turned up today? Anybody riding an IDT bike?'

'What's an IDT bike?' said Kal.

'Like a scrapheap on wheels!' Billy told them.

Tib and Kal looked at each other. Then nodded.

Sandy's hopes began to rise. 'What did they look like?'

'Like scrapheaps on wheels!' said Kal.

'The riders, not the bikes,' Billy sighed.

'One had a long straggly beard that kept getting caught in the front wheel,' said Tib.

'Canticle!' yelled Billy.

'What about the other one?' Sandy asked.

'Seriously weird!' said Tib. 'Had windows on his nose.'

'Windows?' Billy snorted. 'Nobody wears windows on their nose.'

But Sandy knew better. 'Brains does!' she said. 'Brains wears windows. They mean his glasses.' She grabbed hold of Grenville and gave him a hug. 'It's Brains, Grenville. They've seen Brains.'

Grenville howled with pleasure.

'Which way did the bike riders go?' Sandy asked.

Tib pointed down the road. 'The Beard in the Wheel went that way.'

Kal pointed up the road. 'The Windows on the Nose went that way.'

Sandy pulled Billy and Grenville to one side. 'We'll go after Brains,' she told them. 'We'll soon catch up with him if we get the bus.'

Billy turned back to Tib and Kal. 'Think the bus will be here soon?' he said.

Tib and Kal scratched their cobwebs.

'Hard to say.'

'That's not much help,' Sandy told them. 'Can't you give us a better idea?'

'Well,' said Tib. 'I'd say a bus will come along just as soon as somebody invents it.'

Billy's head was starting to spin. 'You mean nobody's invented a bus yet?'

Tib shook his head. A spider fell to the floor and started the long crawl back up a thread of web.

'In that case, what's this bus stop doing here?' Billy demanded.

'Same as us. Waiting for a bus to be invented,' said Kal.

'But what use is a bus stop without a bus?' Billy was getting angry now.

'And what use is a bus without a bus stop?' Kal replied.

'I've had enough of this,' said Billy.

Billy stalked off along the road. Grenville looked up at Sandy.

'We'd better go,' Sandy told Tib and Kal. 'We're in a rush. Thanks for the help. Hope you don't have to wait too long.'

'It doesn't matter. We'll only have to wait for something else after that,' said Tib. Or was it Kal? That's the trouble with identical friends. You can't tell one from the other.

For hour after hour, Billy, Sandy and Grenville tramped the long, dusty road. But there was no sign of Brains. At the bottom of the twenty-first hill – or it might have been the twenty-second – Billy sank to the ground.

'I can't go on. I'm starving,' he moaned.

Grenville was starving as well. He licked Billy's leg. It tasted good. If only he'd had some tomato sauce.

Billy pushed him away.

'Well there's nothing to eat here,' said Sandy. 'So we might as well keep going.'

Sandy dragged Billy to his feet and they set off up the hill. At the top a surprise was waiting for them. Down in the valley was a town. And in a field just outside the town were the brightly coloured lights of a fairground.

Grenville sniffed the breeze.

So did Sandy and Billy.

'Can you smell burger and chips?' asked Sandy.

There was no reply. Billy and Grenville were already racing down the hill towards the fairground.

A sign over the entrance said:

GIANT FAIR AND CIRCUS.
ENTRANCE FREE. PAY ON THE WAY OUT.

Sandy read the sign. 'Pay on the way out! That's crazy.'

'Who cares?' said Billy. 'All those in favour of going in, raise your hands.'

The smell of burger and chips was mixed with the smell of hot doughnuts.

Sandy and Billy put up two hands each. Grenville lay on his back and put up four paws.

'That's it then,' said Sandy. 'In we go.'

And in they went. It was a big mistake.

The fairground was packed with people. Pushing and shoving. Laughing and joking. Shouting and yelling people. All trying to get to their favourite stall. To play their favourite game. To win their favourite prize. It was like every fair you've ever seen. Except that it wasn't. Not when you looked closely.

At one of the stalls a red-faced man with a nose like a pickled cucumber grabbed Billy.

'Have a go at this,' he said.

'What do I have to do?' said Billy.

'Throw a goldfish into a bowl.'

Cucumber nose thrust a bucket of goldfish towards him.

'Throw a goldfish into a bowl?' said Billy. 'What for?'

'To win a prize.'

'What prize?'

'Shiny new ping-pong ball. Marvellous pets ping-pong balls. They live forever. And you never have to feed them.'

Billy pulled himself away.

'No thanks,' he said. 'I'm not allowed pets.'

There was an excited crowd round the next stall.

'Roll up, roll up,' a woman was shouting. 'Catch a crab and win a prize.'

There was a large glass tank. Full of angry looking crabs.

'Come along now. Nice big crabs. Lovely sharp claws. A prize every time.'

'I'll have a go,' said a man in the crowd. He thrust his hand down into the tank. There was a snapping of claws and a tortured yell of pain.

'Look! I got one!' he bawled. A crab with claws like garden shears was dangling from his finger. 'What's the prize?'

'A sore finger!' shouted the woman.

The crowd screamed with delight.

'Oh boy!' said Sandy. 'This is one freaky fair.'

And it got worse. There was the Coconut Shy where the coconuts hid behind the stands because they were too shy to show themselves. The Ghost Train that only ghosts were allowed to ride on. And the Helter Skelter where you put your mat at the bottom and tried to slide up.

It was all so strange that Billy, Sandy and Grenville forgot about the hunger that was nagging away inside them. Then Grenville caught a whiff of waffles wafting on the wind. His ears stood up. His eyes bulged. His tail shot out. And his nostrils went to work.

He cut through the crowd like a bullet from a gun. The smell of waffles dragged him forward like a giant magnet. Until finally – disappointment. The owner of the Waffle Stall was just shutting up.

'Back in ten minutes,' he told them. 'It's time for the Battle of the Borang-Urilla. Can't miss that.'

Nobody wanted to miss that. Everybody was

heading towards one corner of the fairground where a mass of floodlights was lighting up a small wooden stage.

'The Battle of the Borang-Urilla?' said Sandy. 'Wonder what it is?'

'Let's find out,' said Billy.

The famished friends pushed their way to the front of the crowd.

On stage was an empty cage. A metal door split it into two halves.

'Wonder what it's for?' said Sandy.

They soon found out.

A man with a straw hat and a stripy shirt climbed onto the stage.

'Ladies and Gentlemen,' he bawled. 'Welcome to the fight of the century. The Battle of the Borang-Urilla. Brought to you by the Great Grazzo.'

At the side of the stage stood a man like a bald barrel on legs. On his face he wore a toothbrush moustache, caterpillar eyebrows and an evil grin. Next to him was a soppy looking beanpole in pyjamas. The barrel on legs bowed to the crowd.

The crowd gave a half-hearted boo.

'Crikey!' Billy gulped. 'That's them. Grazzo and Squirm!'

On stage the straw hat was speaking again.

'In the right cage, I give you – the Borang-Urilla!'

The crowd gasped as a trap door opened and the Borang-Urilla rose into view. How do you describe a Borang-Urilla? It was like a cross between a baboon, a gorilla and an orang-utang. But not so pretty. It had hands that could crush rocks. And a look on its face that would make your knees knock, if they hadn't already turned to jelly. It was not an animal that you would cheat at cards.

The crowd took one step backwards. Nobody wanted to be too near the Borang-Urilla. Even if it was in a cage.

The man in the straw hat and stripy shirt waited until the Borang-Urilla stopped banging the bars of the cage. 'And now in the left cage tonight's challenger – Glass Eyes, the Borang-Urilla's dinner.'

A trap door in the floor of the left cage opened. And up popped a small, frightened looking figure. Known in the Land of Badlidrempt as Glass Eyes. But known to his friends as –

'Brains!' Sandy gulped. 'They've got Brains!'

Some of the crowd turned to look at her.

'What was that?' demanded the man from the waffle stall.

Billy answered. 'They've got brains. Making the Borang-Urilla fight a wimp like that. He's bound to win.'

Waffle Stall grunted and turned back to the stage.

Straw and Stripy was at it again. 'Now, some of you might think this is not a fair fight. So to make it fairer I am giving the Glass Eyes a pair of boxing gloves.'

The crowd roared with laughter. Grazzo guffawed. Squirm sniggered. Even the Borang-Urilla chuckled behind his hand. Only Billy, Sandy, Brains and Grenville couldn't see the joke.

Straw and Stripy was coming to an end. 'Ladies and gentlemen, only the metal door is between the Glass Eyes and the Borang-Urilla. Ten seconds after I press this button the door will open and the fight will begin.'

The crowd grew hushed. Brains tried to escape through the bars of the cage. The Borang-Urilla licked its lips and looked round for the salt and pepper.

'We've got to do something, Billy,' Sandy hissed.

The man in the straw hat and stripy shirt pressed the button and the clock began to tick.

Brains was ten seconds away from having dinner with a Borang-Urilla. And only one of them would be having pudding.

# Chapter 6

—

'Ten!' counted the crowd. 'Nine! Eight!…'

'We've got to do something, Billy,' said Sandy.

'But what?'

'Seven! Six!…' Time was running out.

Sandy's head was in a spin.

'Five!'

Then Sandy had it. 'The clock!' she yelled.

'Four!'

'Stop the clock and the door won't open.'

'Three!'

'Come on!' yelled Sandy.

'Two!'

Sandy, Billy and Grenville scrambled onto the stage.

'One!'

They dived for the clock and grabbed the finger. The clock stopped. The door stayed shut.

'Zer....Ohhhh!' The crowd groaned with disappointment.

'Made it!' shouted Sandy.

There was a stunned silence. For a second nobody moved. Then Grazzo leapt forward.

'Get them!' he roared.

'Yes. Be getting them,' Squirm squealed.

Three keepers were at the side of the stage. They had a huge net in case the Borang-Urilla escaped. They ran forward. The net sailed through the air. The next moment it came down. Trapping Billy, Sandy and Grenville where they stood.

Frantically they struggled. But the more they struggled the more tangled they became.

Then they heard a voice shout.

'Bite through the net, Grenville.' It was Brains.

Grenville didn't need telling twice. Again and again he ripped at the net. Until at last it parted and he struggled free.

'Run for it, Grenville,' Brains shouted.

Grenville looked around. How could he run for it? The crowd was blocking his way. Grenville stared at the crowd. The crowd stared at Grenville.

'Go Grenville! Go!'

Grenville bared his teeth and snarled.

The crowd gulped.

Grenville leapt from the stage.

The crowd ran for it.

'The Hairy Creature, Squirm!' bellowed Grazzo. 'Grab the Hairy Creature.'

But the Hairy Creature had gone. Disappeared into the distance. Escaped.

'Good old Grenville,' Sandy shouted. 'You'll never catch him now.'

'Silence!' Grazzo roared.

'Silence yourself!' said Billy.

Grazzo glared at Billy. 'One more sound and the Great Grazzo will tie up your tongue and feed you to the Nine Legged Wortle!'

'Oh heck!' said Billy.

'That was one more sound, Grazzo,' Squirm pointed out. 'Feed him to the Wortle now.'

'Shut up, Squirm! Or I will be feeding you to the Wortle as well.'

Squirm shut up.

But Sandy yelled out, 'Hey you! Fatso Grazzo!'

A huge grin spread across Grazzo's face. 'Fatso!' he said. 'The Red Hair called me fatso.'

'But you are a fatso, Grazzo,' wheedled Squirm.

'Oh Squirm!' Grazzo almost blushed.

'Is true, Grazzo. You are the most amazingly corpulent. The most fattest man in the land. And also – the biggest ugly.'

Grazzo's eyes sparkled. 'No, no,' he simpered. 'You just try to flatter me.'

'No, he doesn't,' shouted Sandy. 'You are ugly. Even more ugly than the Borang-Urilla.'

The Borang-Urilla looked hurt.

'And you've got the brains of an overripe tomato!' Sandy continued. 'Now let us out of here or – '

'Or what?' thundered Grazzo.

Sandy thought for a moment. 'Or you'll wish you had!' It wasn't much of a threat. But it was the best she could come up with.

The crowd giggled then cheered wildly as Grazzo said, 'Take them to the dungeons. Tomorrow they appear in the Circus ring. To battle with the Seven Headed Zaldir.'

The crowd were still cheering as Billy, Sandy and Brains were bundled off towards the dungeons. Only the Borang-Urilla was disappointed. He'd gone without his dinner.

The dungeons were dark, damp and deep underground.

Sandy, Billy and Brains huddled together in a corner and told the stories of what had happened to them.

Brains had been riding along the road when

a gang of thugs jumped out on him. They handed him over to Grazzo.

'What about the IDT bike?' asked Sandy.

'Grazzo took it,' sighed Brains. 'It could be anywhere.'

'Oh great!' said Billy. 'So now we've got no bike at all. We're never going to get home.'

Brains tried to look on the bright side. 'Never give up, Billy,' he said. 'Don't forget that only a couple of hours ago I was going to be the Borang-Urilla's dinner.'

'Yes,' said Billy glumly. 'And now we're all going to be the Seven Headed Zaldir's breakfast.'

'No,' said Sandy. She jumped to her feet. 'We'll escape. Brains can pick the lock on the door.'

'There isn't a lock,' Billy told her. 'It's bolted. On the outside. And you can't pick bolts.'

'We could try breaking it down,' Brains suggested.

'We'd need a battering ram,' said Sandy. 'Something big and heavy.'

'We could use Billy,' said Brains. 'He's big and heavy.'

Billy started to back away across the cell. 'Oh no! I'm not being bashed head first against the door.'

'Not head first,' said Brains. 'Feet first.'

But Billy wasn't going to be used as a battering ram. Head first or feet first.

'Just forget it,' he said firmly.

'So you'd rather come face to face to face to face to face to face to face with the seven headed Zaldir would you?'

Billy thought for a moment. 'Yes,' he said.

Brains shrugged. 'We wouldn't have been able to lift him anyway.'

Billy breathed a sigh of relief and sat down again. 'When are they going to feed us?' he wondered.

'Tomorrow,' said Sandy. 'They're going to feed us to the Seven Headed Zaldir.'

'I mean when are we going to get some food?'

Billy's question was answered almost immediately. The bolts slid back. The door creaked open. And the Jailer peeped inside.

'It's only me,' he croaked. He had a voice like a frog with a sore throat. But he looked more like a toad with mumps. 'I've brought some food.'

'About time,' said Billy. 'What is it?'

'Three slices of mouldy bread and a jug of smelly water!'

The Jailer put a tray on the floor and slid it across the cell.

'Are you sure you can spare it?' asked Brains.

'You're lucky,' the Jailer told him. 'I should only give you one slice of mouldy bread and a glass of smelly water.'

Billy picked up a slice of mouldy bread. 'I bet even the Seven Headed Zaldir gets better food than this.'

The Jailer shook his head. 'The Zaldir isn't getting any supper,' he said. 'He'll be having a big breakfast.'

The big breakfast looked at each other.

'Which one of us is the cornflakes?' said Billy.

The Jailer checked outside the door. Then he whispered. 'I've got something to tell you. About the Zaldir.'

Billy, Sandy and Brains drew nearer.

'You have only one chance of staying alive.'

'Yes,' said Billy. 'Run like mad.'

'No,' said the Jailer. 'Do not move. The Zaldir shoots out his tongues to catch his prey. Like a lizard catching a fly. But this one is old and almost blind. If you do not move he will not see you. Believe me.'

'Why should we?' asked Sandy. 'You work for Grazzo, don't you?'

'Grazzo forces us to work for him. Everyone hates him. He is cruel and evil. But those who cross him end up in the Circus Ring. And that's certain death.'

The Jailer left.

Billy, Sandy and Brains gulped.

Certain death!

'Oh well,' said Sandy bravely. 'At least Grenville got away.'

'Good old Grenville,' said Brains.

Billy nodded. Secretly he wished that he'd got away and Grenville had been caught. He took a bite of mouldy bread. It tasted awful. No butter. 'You could get ill eating that,' Brains told him.

'Good! Then I'll give the Zaldir a pain in the stomach as well.'

They ate the mouldy bread and drank the smelly water.

They spent the rest of the night trying to stand still.

First thing the next morning, the bolts slid back and the cell door opened. Two guards entered.

'Where's the Jailer?' asked Sandy.

'You'll see him later at the Circus.' One of the guards grinned. 'Now come on. Don't want to keep the Seven Headed Zaldir waiting for his breakfast.'

Billy, Sandy and Brains were marched along corridors and up stairs. Until they came to an iron barred gate. On the other side of the gate was the Circus Ring.

Billy, Sandy and Brains peered through the bars of the gate.

Most circuses are held in tents. Not Grazzo's. It was a huge stadium big enough to hold thousands of people. And today it was packed. Standing room only.

It was always standing room only. There were no seats. Only Grazzo and Squirm were allowed to sit down. They had their own special place right next to the ring.

From there, they watched to make sure nothing went wrong. The events were already underway.

'Next is the turn of the Glass Eyes, the Red Hair and the Other One to fight the Seven Headed Zaldir,' Squirm told Grazzo.

'Squirm!' Grazzo snapped. 'Shut up! I am watching the Crocogator Tank.'

Out in the middle of the ring was a tank of water the size of a small swimming pool. In it a dozen or more angry, hungry Crocogators snapped, twisted and turned. Above them a wire stretched between two posts. Someone was standing at the end of the wire. About to walk the tightrope over the Tank of Crocogators.

'Another most brilliantest of ideas, Grazzo,' Squirm said. 'To make a man walk the tightrope over the Crocogator tank.'

The crowd agreed. It grew hushed as the tightrope walker slid one foot onto the wire. Squirm covered his eyes and peeped through his fingers. He wasn't as bloodthirsty as he made out.

From behind the gate, Sandy, Billy and Brains watched in horror as the second foot slid onto the wire.

'You know, Sandy,' Brains whispered. 'I've seen that tightrope walker somewhere before.'

Sandy and Billy took a long hard look. Suddenly they realised who it was.

'So that's why they said we'd see him later,' gasped Billy.

Through his fingers on the other side of the stadium Squirm was also taking a good hard look.

'Grazzo!' he wheedled. 'The tightrope man. He looks like the Jailer.'

'It is the Jailer,' Grazzo grinned. 'He tried to help the Glass Eyes. And nobody double crosses the Great Grazzo and lives.'

But the Jailer was doing well. Already he was half way along the tightrope.

'I think he's going to get there,' said Sandy.

The crowd started to grumble. They thought he was going to get there as well. And that wasn't what they'd come to see. It wasn't what Grazzo had come to see either. He signalled to a guard standing next to the tank. The guard grabbed one of the posts and shook it.

The wire bounced up and down. For a moment, the Jailer kept his balance. He leaned to the right. Back to the left. Then right again. But it was hopeless. His foot slipped. His hands grabbed for the wire. They missed. He hit the water in a flurry of arms and legs. His head rose to the surface then he disappeared in a tangle of snapping Crocogator jaws. The crowd cheered. Squirm went white. Grazzo bowed. And Sandy, Billy and Brains groaned.

The next minute, the gate flew open. They were pushed into the ring. And the gate clanged shut.

'Remember!' Sandy hissed. 'Nobody move!'

The crowd was silent. This was what everyone had come to see. The battle of the funny looking strangers against the Seven Headed Zaldir.

Billy, Sandy and Brains were alone in the ring. The guards had gone. Nobody wanted to be within reach of the dreaded Zaldir's tongue.

From his private box Grazzo raised a hand. At the far end of the ring a huge wooden door rumbled open and there stood – the Seven Headed Zaldir.

Someone once said that the Seven Headed Zaldir was not the most terrifying creature in Badlidrempt. That the Eight Headed Zaldir was far more frightening. But the Eight Headed Zaldir only had three tongues. And teeth as sharp as kitchen knives. The Seven Headed Zaldir had a full set of tongues. And teeth like razors. Either way, neither of them made good house pets. They put their heads through the roof. Made enormous messes on the carpet. And ate their owners. Perhaps that's why they were dying out.

The Zaldir lumbered forward. Its seven heads weaved from side to side on its seven necks. And every few moments its seven tongues flicked out one after the other.

'As still as statues,' Sandy hissed.

Billy and Brains froze.

The Zaldir sniffed the air as it stumbled

blindly forward towards the centre of the ring. The crowd held its breath.

The Zaldir stopped. Its tongues flicked out. Nearer this time.

The crowd yelled for the Zaldir to carry on.

A few more paces.

The crowd cheered. Now the Zaldir was within striking distance. Excited by the noise it opened its mouths and bellowed.

Billy, Sandy and Brains felt the withering blast of its hot breath. A nose curling smell filled the air. The stench of rotting meat, month-old socks, dustbin lids and boiled cabbage all rolled into one. It was a stink that a thousand cans of air freshener couldn't wipe out. A whiff you would run a hundred miles to escape from. But Billy, Sandy and Brains stood their ground.

The Zaldir bellowed again. Then turned away.

The plan was working. As long as they kept still the Zaldir could not see them. The Jailer had been right.

The crowd sensed that something was wrong.

The Zaldir sensed that something was wrong.

Even Squirm sensed that something was wrong.

He started to panic. 'Grazzo! Why is the Zaldir not doing the attacks?'

'They do not move. So he does not see them,' Grazzo replied.

The crowd hooted and shook their fists. They put out their tongues and waggled them up and down. And they shoved their thumbs in their ears and flapped their fingers. That was a sign that they were getting really angry.

Squirm was shaking with fear. 'Grazzo, what do we be doing? The crowd is not happy.'

But Grazzo was not worried. He was ready for this. He reached under his seat and took out a brown paper bag filled with sneezing powder. With a flick of the wrist Grazzo sent it flying into the ring. It burst open just in front of Billy. The powder flew up into the air. And Billy's nose started to twitch.

'Keep still, Bill,' Sandy warned through tightened teeth. 'Keep still and we'll be all right.'

But Billy wasn't all right. The sneezing powder was doing its job. Billy's nose was about to explode.

'Sandy!' he said. 'I can feel a sneeze coming on.'

Billy's nostrils were quivering uncontrollably.

'Don't sneeze, Billy!' Brains ordered. 'If you sneeze the Zaldir will see you.'

But the sneeze was on its way. There was no way of stopping it. It was only a matter of time. Billy knew it. Sandy and Brains knew it. Grazzo and Squirm knew it. Even the crowd knew it. Only the Seven Headed Zaldir didn't know it. And it was about to find out.

# Chapter 7

—

All eyes were on Billy as he battled against the sneeze.

'There can be no stopping the sneeze now, Grazzo,' said Squirm.

Grazzo beamed with delight. His plan was working.

Then a strange look came over his face. Someone was licking his leg. And there was a funny rumbling noise down near his feet.

'Squirm,' Grazzo shuddered. 'Is it you that is licking my leg and making the rumbly bumbly noises?'

'No, Grazzo.'

'Then what is it, Squirm?'

Squirm glanced down. 'It is the Hairy Creature, Grazzo.'

'The Hairy Creature? The friend of the Glass Eyes, the Red Hair, and the other one?'

'Yes, Grazzo. And he is showing his big sharp teeth to your leg.'

Grenville opened his mouth and sank his big sharp teeth into Grazzo's leg.

'OOOOOOOoooowwww!' Grazzo yodelled. 'My lllleeeeggggg!' He leapt high in the air. But Grenville hung on. He only let go when Grazzo landed again.

'Get out, Squirm!' Grazzo shouted.

There was only one way to go.

They went.

Over the wall and down into the ring. There was a roar from the crowd. The Seven Headed Zaldir was lumbering towards them. It wasn't to say hello!

Grazzo and Squirm raced across the ring. The Seven Headed Zaldir was barely a tongue's length behind.

The crowd screamed with delight.

Sandy, Billy and Brains were amazed. They couldn't understand why Grazzo and Squirm had suddenly leapt into the ring. Then they heard it.

'Woah! Woah!'

And Grenville jumped down into the ring.

'Grenville!' shouted Sandy. 'You saved us!'

'Aaaaatishhhoooo!' sneezed Billy. He couldn't

hold back any longer. But the Zaldir was too busy chasing Grazzo and Squirm to notice.

'Let's disappear,' Brains yelled. 'While nobody's looking.'

The only way out of the Circus Ring was the way the Zaldir had come in. Sandy, Billy, Brains and Grenville sprinted through the opening and into a passageway that led down beneath the stands. Down to the stables where the monstrous animals that fought in the Circus were kept.

Deeper and deeper they went. And as the roar of the crowd faded away, so the howls and cries of the caged beasts grew louder. There was the angry snattle of the Crocogators. The yapping snarl of the Rip-clawed Grizzly Ape. The trumpeting troat of the Sword-horned Rhinosticon. And the full-throated bellowing roar of the Giant Armour-Plated Thrump. (Which protects itself by curling up into a ball the size of an elephant and steamrollering everything in its path.)

By the time they reached the stables themselves the noise was terrifying.

'Let's go back,' shouted Billy above the din.

'No. We've got to go on,' said Sandy. 'Don't worry about the animals. They're all locked up.'

'Then you go first,' Billy told her.

Sandy went first.

The stables were caves. Hollowed out of the rock. Heavy wooden doors kept the miserable beasts locked away. Only allowed out to fight in the ring. Then at the end of a bloody battle those still alive were herded back. Back to the damp, murky gloom.

'I hate Grazzo,' said Sandy. 'Keeping them down here like this. Why don't we let them out?'

'Because they'd eat us!' said Billy. 'Now hurry.'

At the end of the stables the passageway disappeared into the rock. No more lights. It was pitch black.

'Your turn to go first!' said Sandy and pushed Billy in.

Ten paces along, the passage turned right. Billy didn't. He hit the wall, nose first.

'Let Grenville go first,' said Brains.

Grenville sniffed his way forward through the inky blackness. As he sniffed his eyes began to water. What Grenville could sniff was not a nice niff. It was a nasty niff.

'What's that smell?' said Sandy.

'It's Grenville,' said Billy, pushing his fingers up his nose.

'No,' said Brains. 'It smells like sewers.'

Grenville barked his agreement. It did smell like sewers.

They soon found out why. The passageway opened out into a huge brick-lined cavern. An underground river flowed through the cavern. And all the drains from the stadium above emptied into it.

The smell was nose-shrivelling. And there was worse to come. There was an ear-splitting screech and a flapping of wings. And something swooped down at them from the shadows above.

'Look out!' Brains shouted.

Billy, Sandy, Brains and Grenville dropped to the floor. The wings swished just above their heads. Then rose back into the darkness.

'What was that?' said Sandy.

'Some sort of bat,' Brains answered.

'A bat!' said Billy. 'You can't have a bat that size. It was as big as an eagle!'

'Duck!' shouted Sandy.

'Don't be dopey!' Billy said. 'It was nothing like a duck.'

'Duck! Here it comes again!'

The bat swooped. There was a ripping sound and part of Billy's shirt disappeared.

'Hey!' yelled Billy. 'That was my second-best shirt.'

'Get back against the side,' said Brains.

Billy, Sandy, Brains and Grenville flattened themselves against the slimy wall of the cavern.

The bat swooped again. But its wings were too big to get near the wall.

'What's it trying to do?' Sandy asked Brains.

'Isn't that obvious?' he said. 'It's a giant carnivorous bat.'

'What's carnivorous mean?' Billy demanded.

'It eats meat.'

'But we haven't got any meat.'

'We are the meat, stupid!'

'Edge round the wall!' Sandy ordered. 'It can't get us as long as we stay close.'

Billy inched sideways. He didn't inch far. His skull clunked against a metal rail.

'Owwww!' He looked up.

Sticking out from the wall was a metal ladder which disappeared up into the darkness.

'Climb it!' said Brains.

Billy hesitated.

'Climb it!' said Sandy.

Billy wasn't sure.

'Climb it!' yelled Brains and Sandy.

'But what about Grenville?' Billy shouted back. 'He can't climb a ladder!'

'Carry him,' Sandy told Billy.

'No way,' Billy replied.

But it was too late. Brains and Sandy were already draping Grenville across Billy's shoulders.

'Grenville, you eat too much!' Billy groaned. 'I can't climb a ladder with you on my back.'

Grenville growled.

The bat swooped down.

And Billy started to climb. Sandy and Brains followed behind.

Again and again the bat attacked. But at the top of the cavern, the ladder carried on into a kind of chimney too small for the bat to follow. For the moment they were safe.

Up and up they climbed. Until at last they saw a small circle of light above them.

Slowly the circle of light grew bigger. It was sunlight. When they climbed out they were on the roof of the stadium.

'How are we going to get down from here?' Billy gulped.

'Maybe we could slide down a drainpipe,' Brains suggested.

'I'm not sliding down a drainpipe with this

dumpy dog on my back,' Billy announced. He slumped down in a heap.

Grenville had had enough of wrapping himself around Billy's neck. He scrambled down. The roof was slippy with a steep slope. As Grenville's feet hit the surface they went in four different directions.

'Careful, Grenville,' said Brains.

'Ruff!' Grenville was trying to be careful. It wasn't easy.

'There must be some way down,' said Sandy. 'Everybody think!'

There was a way down. Grenville discovered it. He stood up and shook himself. His feet slipped again. But this time they all slipped in the same direction. Down the roof.

'Dopey dog!' said Billy. 'Stop messing about.'

But Grenville wasn't messing about. He was seriously sliding.

'Grab him, Brains!' yelled Sandy.

Brains grabbed him. By the tail. But it didn't stop Grenville sliding. Brains started to slip as well. He reached out and caught hold of Billy's foot.

Billy started to slide with the other two. Sandy dived across and grabbed him by the wrist.

'It's OK,' she shouted. 'I've got you.'

Sandy was wrong. It wasn't OK. She hadn't got them. They'd got her. She clawed at the roof with her free hand but it was no good. They were on the slide and there was no way of stopping.

Like ski jumpers they hurtled closer and closer to the edge. Finally there was no roof left and they found themselves flying through the air. Heading down towards the ground. They were parachute jumping without a parachute.

Four mouths opened. Three voices screamed. One howled. It was going to be a noisy end.

# Chapter 8

---

It had been a difficult day for Humpy Widlow. Humpy was a trucker. He drove a sixteen-wheeled, eight-horsepower, juggernaut hay-cart. It was eight-horsepower because it was pulled by eight horses. It wasn't a job that Humpy enjoyed doing. It gave him the hump. That's why people called him Humpy.

Every day was a misery to him. Have you ever tried driving a sixteen-wheeled haycart down a country lane just wide enough to push a wheelbarrow along? I have. It's not easy. And in towns it's no better. People don't like juggernaut hay carts tearing along the streets at five miles an hour. It's dangerous. And eight horses make a lot of pollution.

To make matters worse, he was running very late. Things had held him up. First, two waiters waiting at a bus stop stopped him. They thought he was a bus. Then he'd been stopped by a bunch of Thugs. They were looking for four prisoners who'd escaped from the Circus.

So as Humpy drove past the Circus Stadium he had the hump worse than ever. He was as bad tempered as a twin-fanged elephant shark with tuskrot.

Then something fell out of the sky and landed on the back of his cart. Humpy screeched to a stop. And went to look.

He didn't like what he saw. There were four holes in his hay.

'What's going on?' yelled Humpy. 'Who's been bombing my cart?'

Four heads popped out of the holes. Four very dazed heads.

'Where are we?' asked Sandy.

'On my hay cart,' snapped Humpy. 'And I'm not happy.'

'I am,' said Billy. 'I'm very happy. I thought we'd had it.'

'So did I!' Brains gasped.

'Woah! Woah!'

Grenville thought they'd had it as well. But they hadn't. They'd hit the hay not the ground. It was much much better.

But Humpy didn't think so. He climbed up

onto the cart. 'You might not have had it yet,'
he threatened. ' But you're going to get it now!'

Grenville growled and bared his teeth.

Humpy climbed down again. Enough bad
things had happened for one day. And the hairy
one with the teeth looked dangerous.

'Sorry about your hay, sir,' said Brains. 'We
didn't mean to squash it. We just happened to
be up on the roof and we –'

Brains had run out of ideas.

'We must've dropped off,' Sandy chipped in.

Humpy scowled up at them. 'Well you can
drop off again,' he said. 'Off my cart.'

'But we can't,' Billy protested. 'We're hiding
from Grazzo and Squirm.'

'Billy!' Sandy and Brains hissed. Nobody was
supposed to know that they were escaping
from Grazzo and Squirm.

But Humpy's eyes lit up. 'Grazzo! I hate
Grazzo.'

'You do?' said Brains.

''Course I do. He's taken over all the bridges
in Badlidrempt. Makes everybody pay to get
across. Juggernaut haycarts pay double. So any
enemy of Grazzo's is a friend of mine.'

'Then we're the best friends you've got,' said
Billy. 'Because we're Grazzo's biggest enemies.'

Humpy drew closer to the cart. 'Tell me,' he said. 'Is Grazzo as nasty as they say? Is he horribly, revoltingly, sickeningly, foully, disgustingly nasty?'

'No!' Sandy shook her head. 'He's worse than that. Now please can we get away from here?'

'Where do you want to go?'

Where did they want to go? Sandy decided. 'The Land of Sorcerers,' she said. 'There's something we've got to get back.'

Sandy was right. If Grazzo had Brains's IDT bike, the only hope they had of getting home was to find Canticle.

Humpy sucked his teeth. 'Land of Sorcerers is an awful long way,' he said. 'I can't take you there. But I can get you started.'

'It's a deal,' said Billy.

'Ruff!' Grenville agreed.

Humpy took a long hard look at him. 'Tell me,' he said. 'Is that a Woolly Sausage?'

'No,' said Sandy. 'It's a Grenville. Now let's go.'

Humpy jumped into the driving seat. It wasn't a bad day after all. He was getting his own back on Grazzo and Squirm. He cracked the whip and the eight-horsepower horses surged forward. Humpy grinned. If it went on like this, people would start calling him Happy, not Humpy.

Sandy, Billy, Brains and Grenville sank down into the hay. A moment later they were asleep.

It had been a close thing but they'd done it. They'd fooled the Seven Headed Zaldir. They'd got away from Grazzo. All they had to do now was find Canticle and the IDT bike. Then they could go home.

If they'd known how hard that was going to be they would never have gone to sleep.

Humpy Widlow brought the juggernaut hay-cart to a stop.

It had been a good journey. Only one hold-up. On a bumpy stretch of road the Grenville bounced right off the back of the cart. Humpy heard the splash as the Grenville landed in a puddle. He stopped. The Grenville was still asleep. That was one tired Grenville. Humpy threw him back into the hay and carried on.

Humpy climbed down from the driving seat and banged on the side of the cart.

'Here we are then,' he shouted.

Four yawning sleepy heads poked out of the hay.

'What's the matter?' Brains yawned.

'This is where you get off,' Humpy told them.

Suddenly, Billy, Sandy, Brains and Grenville were wide awake. They scrambled down and looked around. They were by the side of a wide, fast-flowing river.

'Where are we?' said Sandy.

'This is the Nameless River,' Humpy replied.

'What's it called?' Billy asked.

'It's called the Nameless River.'

'It's not nameless then, is it?' said Billy. 'Not if it's got a name.'

'The name is Nameless,' said Humpy.

Billy opened his mouth to argue but Brains got in first.

'Which way to the Land of Sorcerers?'

'Across the river.'

'Where's the bridge?' asked Sandy.

Humpy sucked his teeth. 'There is a bridge,' he said. 'But Grazzo's in charge of it.'

'That's no good then,' said Sandy.

'So how do we get across?' demanded Billy. 'It's too far to swim.'

'You'll have to find Panatopolis,' said Humpy.

'Who's Panatopolis?'

'You'll see!' Humpy climbed back up onto the juggernaut haycart. 'I better be going. Got to get as far as Skinny Waldo's Kiphouse before it gets dark. Don't want to be out once the moon rises. That's when the Bloodsucking Vampire Moths start to fly.'

'Bloodsucking Vampire Moths!' gulped Brains. 'They don't really suck blood do they?'

'No,' said Humpy. 'Sucking is too slow. They drink it by the bucket full.'

Humpy let off the brake and cracked the whip. The eight-horsepower juggernaut hay-cart rumbled off.

'Just a minute,' Sandy cried out. 'Where do we find Panatopolis?'

'Walk that way!' Humpy pointed upstream.

Sandy, Billy, Brains and Grenville watched as the haycart disappeared into the distance. When it had finally vanished from sight they started walking.

By nightfall there was still no sign of Panatopolis. They spent an uncomfortable night trying to sleep in a hole by the river.

Brains dreamed he was being attacked by a Bloodsucking Vampire Moth. He woke to find Grenville licking his face.

At first light they started walking again. It was almost midday when they spotted it. A hill. But this was no ordinary hill. Because on top of it sat Panatopolis.

Panatopolis was huge. Too big to be a giant. As tall as the tallest skyscraper. As wide as the widest football pitch. And as ugly as – well, he was ugly.

But stranger than that. Panatopolis was crying.

Yes, he sat on top of the hill and wept. Heart-wrenching sobs burst forth from deep inside him. And huge tears flowed down his face in a non-stop stream.

Each tear contained enough water to fill a large swimming pool. Some would have filled two large swimming pools. They dripped off his chin and cascaded down like a waterfall into the river below.

And stranger still the tears were the river.

Panatopolis cried so much that tears from his left eye formed a river that flowed north. And tears from his right eye made a river that flowed south.

It was the saddest sight you could ever see.

'He must be the unhappiest creature in the world,' sighed Brains.

'In the universe,' said Billy.

Grenville howled.

'Shut up, Grenville,' Sandy hissed.

But it was too late. Panatopolis looked down. He raised a titanic hand in a tearful greeting.

'Who are you?' the vast voice boomed out between sobs.

'Brains, Sandy, Billy and Grenville,' said Brains, pointing to Sandy, Billy and Grenville.

'Oh really? My name's Panatopolis. I'm very pleased to meet you.'

Tears gushed out worse than ever.

'You don't look very pleased,' said Billy.

'Billy!' Sandy looked up at Panatopolis. He was ugly but not frightening. 'Excuse me,' she said. 'But is anything the matter?'

Panatopolis sighed a hurricane. He shook his head. 'No,' he replied. 'Everything's fine. Just fine.'

Sandy tried a smile. 'Oh good,' she said. 'It's just that you look a bit sad.'

'Oh, I'm sad all right,' said Panatopolis. 'Very very sad.'

'But why are you so sad?' asked Sandy.

Panatopolis moaned in despair. 'Why?' he repeated. 'I'm sad because I keep crying all the time. Wouldn't you be sad if you were crying all the time?'

'I expect we would,' said Brains. 'But why are you crying?'

'I'm crying because I'm sad,' Panatopolis told him.

Sandy, Billy, Brains and Grenville thought about this.

'So you're sad because you're crying. And you're crying because you're sad?' said Sandy.

'That's right,' Panatopolis howled. 'I'm so glad you understand. That makes me very happy indeed.' Panatopolis sobbed as though his heart would burst.

'He's round the bend,' Billy announced. 'He just cries all the time.'

But Brains had an idea. 'If we could make him laugh, that would stop him crying. Then the river would dry up. And we could get to the other side.'

Sandy looked up at Panatopolis. He was a perfect picture of misery. 'We can try,' she said. But she wasn't very hopeful. 'I mean, how do we make him laugh?'

'Tell him some jokes,' said Brains.

Billy stepped forward. 'Leave this to me,' he said.

Every Christmas Billy learnt the jokes inside every Christmas cracker he could find. If anybody could make Panatopolis laugh it was him. At least that's what Billy thought.

He cleared his throat. 'Here! Panatopolis! Listen! I've got some jokes for you.'

'Oh good,' Panatopolis sobbed. 'I like jokes. Are they funny ones?'

'The funniest,' said Billy. 'Here's one. Why do birds fly south in winter?…Because it's too far to walk.'

Billy stepped back and waited for the laugh. It never came.

The tears carried on flowing.

'Not even a smile,' said Brains.

'That was the warm up,' Billy told him. 'To get him in the right mood.'

He stepped forward again.

'What's the biggest mouse in the world?…The hippopotamouse!'

No reaction.

Billy carried on.

'Where do tadpoles turn into frogs?…In a croakroom.'

Nothing.

'What do you get if you cross a sheep with a kangaroo?…A woolly jumper.'

Panatopolis sobbed louder than ever.

'Crikey!' said Billy. 'This is hard work.'

'Don't give up, Bill,' Sandy said. 'He's bound to laugh sometime.'

Billy nodded. 'This one'll get him. Hey, Panatopolis! What's black and white and red all over?'

For a second the sobbing stopped. 'A news-paper,' said Panatopolis. 'That's black and white and read all over.'

Billy shook his head. This one always caught them out. He couldn't wait to deliver the punchline.

'No! It's a sunburnt penguin! That's black and white and red all over.'

Billy started to laugh.

Sandy, Brains and even Grenville looked up hopefully at Panatopolis.

Oh yes,' he sobbed. 'That's very funny. Very funny indeed.' But the waterfall of tears was heavier than ever.

This made Billy laugh even more. He chuck-led. He guffawed. He staggered around blindly, clutching his aching sides and hooting with merriment. Finally he fell backwards into the river. That shut him up.

As his head came to the surface Sandy and Brains started to laugh. Billy shook his fist and made a strange gurgling sound. Sandy and Brains screamed with delight. Grenville rolled on his back and kicked his legs in the air.

A fountain of water spouted from Billy's mouth. 'Pull me out,' he choked.

Brains reached down and pulled Billy out.

'Oh Billy,' Sandy giggled. 'You do look funny.'

Billy glared. He took off his shoe and tipped out a half-litre of water.

Brains and Grenville put their heads together and howled.

That just made Billy angrier. He stamped his feet. He should have put his shoe back on first. His bare foot landed on a sharp stone. He hopped around and yowled at the top of his voice.

Sandy, Brains and Grenville laughed even more. Their peals of laughter rolled down the hill. Then another sound began. A deep throaty chuckle that rumbled around the sky.

Sandy, Brains and Grenville stopped laughing. Billy stopped yowling. They couldn't believe it. Panatopolis was laughing. The sight of Billy leaping around dripping wet and clutching his foot had done the trick.

The chuckle grew into a chortle. The chortle into a cackle. The cackle into a full blown belly laugh. And as he laughed the tears of sadness grew fewer and finally dried up altogether.

Immediately, a strip of dirty brown mud appeared. The river bed! This was the chance they'd been waiting for.

Sandy jumped down. 'Come on! Let's get across before he starts crying again.'

Billy thrust his foot into his shoe and scrambled down after her. Brains and Grenville slid down behind.

They were half-way across when things began to go wrong. First, Billy's foot sank down into the mud and got trapped between two stones. He tugged and tugged but it stayed trapped.

Panatopolis thought it was hilarious. He threw back his head and howled uncontrollably. In fact, he laughed so much that he started to cry with laughter.

A first tear rolled down his cheek and splashed to the floor.

Billy, Sandy, Brains and Grenville looked up in alarm. More tears of laughter were falling. Suddenly it was raining swimming pools again. And the river bed was filling with water.

Sandy and Brains grabbed hold of Billy's leg and pulled. It wouldn't budge. It was stuck tight. Already water was lapping at their ankles.

Only four things were certain. Billy was trapped. Panatopolis was still laughing. The water was rising. And time was running out.

# Chapter 9

——

Time had almost run out. The water was up to Grenville's ears. And Grenville couldn't swim. But was he scared?

Yes, he was. Almost as scared as Billy.

The terrified two watched as Sandy and Brains tugged at Billy's foot.

'We need more time,' Brains announced. 'We've got to stop Panatopolis laughing.'

'That's no good,' Sandy snapped. 'He'll just start crying then because he's sad.'

Brains was beaten. Billy was stunned. And Grenville was underwater. Only the tip of his nose was above the surface. It was time for his party trick. He stood up on his hind legs and danced the hokey-cokey. It looked silly but it was better than drowning. Only it made Panatopolis laugh even more. His teardrops were the size of small lakes!

The water was up to Billy's chest. If anybody

was going to have a bright idea, now was the time to have it.

It hit Sandy like a flash of lightning.

'Make him think!' she yelled. 'That will stop him crying.'

'Think about what?'

'Ask him a riddle.'

Panatopolis stopped laughing.

'Did someone say riddles?' he said. 'I love riddles.'

Tears were still falling but they were down to bathtub size. It looked promising. But there was a problem. Nobody knew any riddles.

'I'll just have to make one up,' said Brains. His brain was working at top speed. Sandy thought she could see it flashing behind his eyes. But it was just the sun reflecting on his glasses.

'Got one!' he shouted after seven and a half seconds.

'What occurs once in a minute? Twice in a moment? But never in a thousand years?'

Instantly the crying stopped. The eyes dried up. And the brain started to work.

'What occurs once in a minute? Twice in a moment? But never in a thousand years?' Panatopolis wondered.

Already the water was getting lower.

Soon Grenville would be able to stop the hokey-cokey and stand on all fours again.

'Once in a minute. Twice in a moment. But never in a thousand years?' Panatopolis repeated. 'That's hard.'

'Keep thinking. You'll get it,' Brains shouted up to him.

Panatopolis kept thinking. He kept thinking while Sandy and Brains reached down into the soft, sticky mud. He carried on thinking while they freed Billy's foot. And he was still thinking as Billy, Sandy, Brains and Grenville squelched their way across the rest of the muddy river bed.

It was only as they reached the far side that Panatopolis realised what was happening.

'Hey!' he shouted after them. 'What are you doing?'

'Going to get our bike back,' yelled Billy.

'But you can't go,' Panatopolis boomed. 'What about the riddle? I don't know the answer.'

'Shall I tell him?' Brains asked.

'No,' said Sandy. 'We might need to get back across some time.'

As Sandy, Billy, Brains and Grenville hurried off, a huge sad voice shouted after them. 'Please come back. I've got to know the answer. You're making me very very sad.'

The tears were flowing faster than ever. It looked as though there was going to be a flood.

There is an old saying in the Land of Badlidrempt. 'He who searches for the Land of Sorcerers would do better if he had a map, or if he knew where he was going.' It was a stupid saying. But it was very true.

Sandy, Billy, Brains and Grenville didn't know where they were going. And they didn't have a map. So they were glad when they found the signpost.

Billy ran ahead to see what it said. It didn't say anything. Even in Badlidrempt signposts don't talk. But it did have things written on it.

There were four pointers. To the left was Happy Village. To the right was Doom Castle.

'I don't fancy that,' said Sandy. 'What about straight ahead?'

'Somewhere Else Very Nasty.'

'What do you mean?'

'That's what's written on it,' Billy insisted. 'Straight ahead – Somewhere Else Very Nasty. And behind us – Back Where You've Just Come From.'

'So where do we go?' asked Brains.

Well, where would you have gone?

The road to Happy Village was all downhill. Except for the bits of road that were uphill. It was a twisty-turny sort of road with thick bushes on one side and thin bushes on the other. It was a also a happy sort of road.

It made Sandy, Billy, Brains and Grenville glad to be alive. Even though they were still stuck in the Land of Badlidrempt.

They wouldn't have been glad if they'd known what was waiting for them round the next corner.

Two thugs with big wooden clubs. The kind of clubs that were just right for bashing people on the head with. One of the thugs was called Boggle. The other was called Skulk. The clubs were just called clubs.

Boggle and Skulk had spotted Billy, Sandy, Brains and Grenville soon after they crossed the Nameless River. They knew it was them because of the posters. What posters?'

The posters that had been sent out to every town and village in Badlidrempt. The posters that said:

'WANTED.

ALIVE OR NOT SO ALIVE.

THE GLASS EYES, THE HAIRY CREATURE,
THE RED HAIR AND THE OTHER ONE.
REWARD.
MORE MONEY THAN NOTHING
IF YOU'RE LUCKY.
CONTACT THE GREAT GRAZZO
OR ELSE.

Some people thought that Else was Grazzo's sister. But it wasn't. It was just Grazzo's way of saying that anybody who didn't help him capture the Glass Eyes, the Hairy Creature, the Red Hair and the Other One would be in big trouble.

That was why Boggle and Skulk were hiding behind a clump of thick bushes. With their clubs.

'Right, Boggle,' said Skulk. 'This is the plan.'

Boggle listened.

'We hide behind these thick bushes. Then when they go past we jump out. And badonk, badonk.'

'What's badonk?' asked Boggle.

'It's us bashing them on the head with our clubs,' Skulk told him.

'Badonk? Badonk?' Boggle looked puzzled. 'But that's only two badonks. Are we only going to bash two of them?'

'No, you thick-headed thug. We'll bash all of them.'

'Badonk! Badonk! Badonk! Badonk!'

'That's right. Now be quiet. They'll be here soon.'

Boggle and Skulk waited.

They waited.

And they waited some more.

They could have waited for ever. Billy, Sandy, Brains and Grenville had already gone past. Boggle and Skulk hadn't seen them because the bushes were too thick.

'Now what do we do?' said Skulk.

'Hide behind the thin bushes,' Boggle said.

'Don't be a mug, thug,' Skulk told him. 'If we hide behind thin bushes they'll see us.'

'You think of a plan then,' said Boggle.

Skulk did.

Ten minutes later, Brains, Grenville, Sandy and Billy walked round a bend in the road and stopped. A large man with two cauliflower ears and a turnip nose was lying on the ground. There was a club by his side. He didn't look well. And he was moaning.

'Moan!' he said in a loud voice. 'Moan! Moan!'

'He's moaning,' said Brains.

'He needs help,' said Sandy.

'Leave this to me,' said Billy. 'I've got a First Aid badge.'

'I know,' said Brains. 'You bought it at a car-boot sale.'

But there was no time for argument. Something had to be done.

'Excuse me, sir,' Sandy asked. 'But is there anything we can do?'

The man stopped moaning. 'Yes,' he whispered. 'Put your heads down here.'

'Why?' asked Billy.

'Because I've got something for you.'

Sandy, Billy, Brains and Grenville put their heads down.

Badonk! Badonk! Badonk! Badonk!

A few minutes later they were on their way to Happy Village. They didn't know anything about it. They were knocked out.

Somebody once asked why Happy Village was called Happy Village. The answer is simple. It was called Happy Village because it was a happy place. Just being there made people happy. Nobody knew why.

Not that Sandy, Billy, Brains and Grenville were very happy when they woke up there. They were very unhappy. They were tied tightly together. And they had bumps on their heads as big as eggs. Easter eggs!

'Where am I?' moaned Billy.

'I dunno,' Sandy groaned. 'But I'm there as well.'

So was Brains. And Grenville. But he was still knocked out. They were in the Mayor's parlour. And they were being watched by the Mayor and the two thugs.

They knew it was the mayor because he had a chain round his neck. Not a gold chain. A paper chain. One left over from Christmas. The people of Happy Village couldn't afford a gold chain. They were happy, not rich.

'Want me to give them another badonk on the bonce, Mr Mayor?' Boggle asked.

The Mayor shook his head. He was looking closely at Sandy. 'You are them, aren't you?'

'Who?' replied Sandy.

The Mayor unrolled a poster.

'Them!' he explained. 'The Glass Eyes, the Hairy Creature, the Red Hair and the Other One.'

Sandy, Billy and Brains stared at the poster in horror.

'That's not us,' Billy blurted out.

'Yes, it is,' said the Mayor. 'And I'm going to

keep you here until Grazzo turns up with the reward.'

'Grazzo!'

At that moment, Sandy, Billy and Brains (but still not Grenville) realised that it was worse than they thought. Not only were they captured. But they were going to be handed over to Grazzo again.

Sandy tried to talk a way out. 'You don't want to hand us over to Grazzo,' she said.

'Oh yes, we do,' the Mayor smiled. 'He'll probably give us lots and lots of money for catching you.'

'He'll probably double-cross you and chuck you in with the Seven Headed Zaldir,' said Billy.

The Mayor thought for a moment. Billy was right. But if Grazzo found out that Happy Village had let his enemies go, he would make it Unhappy Village.

It was a tricky problem. What could he do?

While he was thinking, the door burst open. And a messenger burst in.

'Mr Mayor,' she burst out. 'I've got a message for you.'

The Mayor wasn't surprised. Messengers always had messages. That was their job.

'Who's the message from?' he asked.

'Gopula!'

'Gopula!' the Mayor gasped. His face went white. His eyes grew red. His lips turned blue. His nose stayed more or less the same colour. He was not a happy Mayor. 'What does he want now?'

'Another four!'

'Another four!' the Mayor was shaking. He turned to Boggle and Skulk. 'Go and grab the first four villagers you can find.'

'No good!' the messenger told him. 'The villagers have already heard. They're hiding.'

The Mayor's face went whiter, his eyes grew redder and his lips turned bluer. His nose was still more or less the same colour. But he was shaking like a jelly on a roller coaster. Even his voice was shaky. 'But if I don't send another four up to him, he'll come here and get us.'

The Mayor looked at Boggle, Skulk and the Messenger. They looked at him. Even Boggle could count up to four.

Then the Messenger had an idea. She whispered in the Mayor's ear.

The Mayor stopped shaking and smiled.

He looked at Billy, Sandy, Brains and Grenville. Then he counted them. 'One! Two! Three! Four!'

'Why are you counting us?' asked Billy. But he already knew why.

The Mayor turned to Skulk. 'Chuck them on the cart and take them up to Gopula.' He picked up the Wanted poster and tore it into sixty-three tiny pieces. 'And we'll just hope that Grazzo doesn't find out.'

Skulk grabbed his club.

Badonk! Badonk! Badonk!

Grenville woke up and growled.

Badonk!

He should have stayed knocked out. For the next couple of hours he did. So did Brains, Sandy and Billy.

When they woke they were on the back of a cart. Not a juggernaut haycart. More of a large wheelbarrow pulled by a cross between a donkey and a kangaroo. Every few steps the animal stopped. Boggle cracked the whip. And it leapt forward again. It wasn't a smooth ride. Especially when you were tied up and rolling around in the back.

Billy's head banged against the side of the cart. It left a bump the size of an ostrich egg. Soon he'd have enough for an omelette.

'Where are we now?' Brains groaned.

'On the way to see this Gopula bloke,' Sandy

replied gloomily.

'I wonder what he's like?' said Billy.

'Can't be any worse than Grazzo and Squirm,' Brains said. 'Ruff!' Grenville agreed.

Grenville was right. He was rough.

The cart jerked to a stop. Skulk climbed into the back and untied the ropes.

'Here we are then,' he said. 'Doom Castle!'

# Chapter 10

—

Thunder rumbled around the sky and lightning flashed.

'Doom Castle! I thought you were taking us to see Gopula,' Sandy complained.

'This is where Gopula lives,' snapped Skulk. And he pushed them off the back of the cart.

By the time they hit the ground the cart was already leapfrogging down the hill. Away from Doom Castle.

Brains sat up. The ropes had gone. They were free. Now was their chance to escape.

'Let's get away before this Gopula guy turns up,' he yelled.

A shadow fell across Brains and a finger tapped his shoulder. Brains turned his head. He was staring at the knees of somebody's trousers. He let his eyes rise up. He saw a belt. Then some shirt buttons. A green bow tie. And finally a puffy, red face with bushy eyebrows and bright blue eyes.

The next moment Brains was lifted off his feet and found himself looking right into those bright blue eyes.

'Excuse me, sir,' Brains gulped. 'But are you Mr Gopula?'

'I am,' Mr Gopula replied. 'But just call me Gopula.'

Gopula was not the biggest giant you've ever seen. Panatopolis was ten times bigger. In fact, Gopula was not much taller than a small giraffe on a step ladder. But he did have a strange look to him.

He looked as though somebody had stuck bits of different bodies together with glue. His hands were too big for his arms. His feet too big for his legs. His tongue was too big for his mouth. And his head was too big for everything. Still, I expect his mother loved him. If he had a mother!

The giant lifted Brains higher still.

'What are you doing here?' he growled. The voice was deep and full of menace.

'I'm glad you asked that, sir,' said Brains politely. 'Because we didn't want to disturb you.

But the Mayor of Happy Village made us come.'

'But you don't look like villagers,' said Gopula.

'We're not,' Sandy stood up and looked him in the knees. 'We're travellers.'

Gopula dropped Brains to the ground. He landed on his feet which was good. He also landed on Grenville's feet which was not so good. Grenville howled in pain and hopped around.

Gopula turned to Sandy. 'Did you say travellers?'

Sandy nodded.

'But that's terrible,' Gopula shouted angrily. 'What an awful way to treat travellers.'

He pulled a huge plate of sizzling sausages from his trouser pocket. The Grenville hop stopped.

'You must be starving,' said Gopula. 'Like a sausage?'

'You bet,' said Billy.

He didn't need asking twice. He crammed a sausage into his mouth.

Gopula offered the plate to Sandy and Brains. More sausages disappeared. Finally, Grenville helped out by finishing off the last five sausages in one gulp.

Gopula looked at the empty plate and grinned. 'All gone!' he said. 'Come inside and have some more.'

It was an offer Billy, Sandy, Brains and especially Grenville couldn't resist.

Inside Doom Castle, a table full of sausages was already waiting for them.

Gopula's eyes lit up. 'I love sausages. My favourite food,' he said. 'I eat them all day long.'

Billy, Sandy, Brains and Grenville stood round the table with their tongues hanging out.

'Sit down and tuck in,' Gopula told them kindly.

They sat down and tucked in.

'Have as many as you like.' Gopula seemed like a very kind giant. 'There are plenty more. I make my own, you know.'

'They really are very delicious,' said Brains.

'Delicious,' Sandy agreed. 'What's the recipe?'

'It's a secret,' Gopula grinned. 'But you'll find out soon.'

'Good,' said Billy. 'We'll make our own when we get home.'

Grenville said nothing. He wasn't wasting time while there were still sausages to eat.

Once the sausages were gone, Sandy, Billy, Brains and Grenville sat back and sighed happily.

Gopula looked around. 'Anyone for any more?' he asked.

Billy and Grenville nodded eagerly.

'Just another dozen or two,' said Billy.

'Wow! Wow! Wow!' barked Grenville.

'Or three,' Billy told Gopula.

Gopula banged his foot on the floor and a servant ran in.

'Take these travellers down to the kitchen and make some sausages with them,' the giant told him.

Gopula's eyes gleamed as he watched Billy and Grenville go. 'I'm sure they'll make some very very good sausages,' he said. He licked his lips as though he could already taste them. 'Now, let's play some games.'

'Games?'

'Yes. I love playing games. Almost as much as I love eating sausages.'

'All right then,' said Sandy. 'What shall we play?'

'Snap!' said Gopula.

'I don't like snap,' Brains said.

'Well, I do,' said Gopula. 'So that's what we'll play.'

The giant took out a pack of snap cards. He gave Sandy and Brains a small pile each and kept the big pile for himself.

'You go first,' he told Brains.

Brains put down a sun.

Sandy put down a moon.

Gopula put down another moon.

'Snap!' said Sandy. She reached out to take the cards.

Gopula stopped her. 'No!' he said. 'I wasn't ready. Start again.'

Brains put down a flower.

Sandy put down a tree.

Gopula put down a star.

Brains put down another star.

'Snap!' he yelled.

'That's not snap,' shouted Gopula.

'Two stars!' Brains pointed out.

'Stars don't count,' Gopula told him. 'It says so in the rules.'

'What rules?'

'My rules!' Gopula stared angrily at Brains. 'Start again. And no cheating this time!'

Brains put down a tree.

Sandy put down a flower.

Gopula looked through his cards and picked out a flower. 'SSSSSNNNNNAAAPPPPP!' he thundered at the top of his voice. His hand crashed down onto the cards. There was a splintering of wood and the table collapsed in a heap.

'You've broken it,' said Brains as the dust cleared.

'In that case, I win,' said Gopula.

'Why?' said Brains.

'It's in the rules,' Sandy told him. She was getting the idea of Gopula's games. There was only one rule. Gopula always wins.

'What shall we play now?' asked the giant.

'Something that doesn't need a table,' said Brains.

Gopula thought for a moment. 'We'll play "I Spy",' he said.

The giant glanced round the room.

'It's got to be something we can all see,' said Sandy.

'I know! I know!' snapped Gopula. A big grin spread across his face. 'Got it!' he said. 'I spy with my great big eye something beginning with S.'

'Easy,' said Brains. 'Socks.'

'No,' said Gopula. 'Try again.'

'Shoes?' Brains suggested.

'Try again.'

'Shirt?'

'No!'

'Skin?'

'No!'

'Is it me? Sandy?' said Sandy.

'No!'

'I can't think of anything else,' said Brains.

'Do you give up then?'

'I suppose so.'

'That makes me the winner,' grinned Gopula.

'Yes, you're the winner,' said Sandy. 'Now what was it you spied?'

'It was – sausages!' Gopula announced.

Sandy and Brains looked round the room.

'That's cheating!' Brains complained. 'There aren't any sausages in here.'

'There will be in a minute,' Gopula told him. 'Servant! More sausages!'

The doors opened and a trolley bigger than a snooker table was wheeled in. It was piled high with sausages of all different sizes. From tiny chipolatas to giant bangers as big as a rolled-up carpet.

'Just in time,' Gopula drooled. 'I'm starving. And I love freshly made sausages, don't you?'

Sandy and Brains weren't hungry. The sight of a mountain of sausages dripping with fat put them off. But they didn't say so.

Gopula picked up a fork and sat down

behind the pile of bangers. 'Get stuck in!' he called out.

The sound of chomping told Brains and Sandy that Gopula had got stuck in. The stack of sizzlers was going down fast. Soon Gopula's head appeared over the top of the sausage mountain. Bangers were disappearing into the cavernous mouth faster than coins into a fruit machine. Finally, the giant was down to his last two sausages. But what sausages they were. They had to be the biggest sausages ever made.

'Excuse me. But aren't those sausages a bit too big to swallow at one go?' said Sandy. 'I mean, they're almost as big as me.'

Even as she said it, Sandy knew that something was wrong. Why were those sausages so much bigger than the rest?

'I like big sausages,' said Gopula. 'The bigger the better.'

The sausages were quivering now. Moving about as though they were still alive. Then one of the sausages barked.

Brains and Sandy looked at each other.

The sausage barked again. It wriggled. It twisted. It started to split open. A leg appeared. Then another leg. Then a tail. Then a head. There was no mistaking it. The barking sausage was a dog. Not a hot dog. But a dog named –

'Grenville!' yelled Brains and Sandy.

Grenville turned and attacked the other sausage. The skin of the second sausage split open. And a very sticky Billy rolled out. He jumped to his feet and pointed a finger at Gopula.

'He's a nutter,' he said. 'He's going to eat us. Run for it!'

Sandy and Brains jumped up from their seats. Billy and Grenville jumped down off the trolley. But Gopula had them cornered. He moved menacingly towards them.

'You stay where you are,' Sandy told him. 'You're a horrible nasty giant. And you made Billy and Grenville into sausages.'

'Yes,' growled Gopula. 'And now I'm going to make you into sausages as well.'

The giant darted over to the wall and pulled a lever.

The floor disappeared from under their feet. And the falling four dropped like stones.

They didn't fall far. They landed in a heap on a metal chute. A metal chute that sloped down into the jaws of a huge machine.

'What's going on?' shouted Sandy as they slid towards the machine.

'Don't worry,' answered Gopula from above. 'It's only my mincing machine.'

'Mincing machine!' yelled Billy.

'Not as tasty as being cooked whole,' Gopula admitted. 'But once you're minced you stay minced!'

The machine whirred into life.

'Goodbye now,' chuckled Gopula. 'The next time I see you, you'll be sizzling on a plate.'

# Chapter 11

——

Already Sandy, Billy, Brains and Grenville could see the whirling blades of the mincing machine. They tried to scramble back up the chute but it was hopeless. Even Grenville couldn't get a grip on the shiny metal surface.

'What are we going to do, Brains?' Sandy shouted.

'I think we're going to get minced!'

'Then shove Grenville in first,' shouted Billy. 'His fur might clog the machine up.'

Grenville scrabbled like mad. He wasn't going to be first. Dogs last was his motto. Already he could feel the blast of air from the spinning blades. He yowled in panic.

Sandy, Billy and Brains screamed for help. But the only answer came from above.

'You're wasting your breath,' Gopula

shouted. 'There's nobody here to help. So you might just as well—'

Then three things happened. There was a thud. Gopula stopped speaking. And something heavy crashed to the floor.

The next moment a fourth thing happened. The mincing machine was switched off. The fantastic four were safe. They were not going to be turned into sausage meat after all. And Gopula would have to go hungry.

Billy, Sandy, Brains and Grenville cheered and clapped. And shouted and laughed. And hugged each other. Then they stopped!

Who had saved them?

They looked up.

Two faces grinned down at them. Faces they'd hoped they'd never see again.

'Grazzo and Squirm!' they groaned.

'Yes. It is I, the great Grazzo.'

'And I the not-so-great Squirm!'

'How nice it is to be seeing you once more again.'

'Yes, Grazzo,' Squirm squirmed. 'But even more nicer for them to be seeing you once more again.'

'Shut up, Squirm,' snapped Grazzo. 'And be helping them up out of the mincey-mincey machine.'

'Yes, Grazzo,' said Squirm. Squirm's long spindly arm reached down towards Sandy. But Sandy stayed put.

'What are you going to do with us?' she said.

Grazzo grinned. 'You will be meeting up with an old friend.'

'What old friend?'

'The Seven Headed Zaldir, of course,'

'Oh no!' said Billy. 'We're not coming back for that. Go and boil your head, instead.'

Squirm gasped. Nobody spoke to Grazzo like that and lived.

But Grazzo merely smiled. 'Then the Zaldir will be most not happy. After your last meeting he was soundly whipped for being so stupid. Now he wishes to pay back that debt.'

'Well, tell him to go and boil his heads as well,' yelled Billy. 'All seven of them. Because we are not coming with you. Not now. Not ever. Never.'

'Then there is only one thing for me to be doing,' said Grazzo. 'Goodbye. For ever.'

Grazzo's head disappeared. There were footsteps across the room. The click of a switch. And the blades of the mincing machine began to turn again.

Squirm looked horrified. He reached down towards Sandy.

'Please, be coming now. Before it is too late!'

'OK!' yelled Sandy. 'Stop the machine. We'll come.'

Immediately the mincing machine stopped. And Grazzo's grinning face appeared over the edge of the floor.

'You see, Squirm, they are wanting to see the Zaldir. Get them up.'

'Oh yes, Grazzo. At once, Grazzo.'

One by one Squirm pulled them up.

Grazzo watched. Hands on hips. His eyes gleaming with delight. Now he would get his revenge for what had happened at the Circus.

Behind him on the floor lay the huge bulk of Gopula. He was still flat out.

'You see,' said Grazzo. 'There is no one that the Great Grazzo cannot defeat.' He threw Squirm a coil of rope. 'Be tying them up, Squirm. The Hairy Creature first. He is the most dangerous.'

Grenville growled and bared his teeth. But Squirm was too quick for him. A loop of rope tightened around Grenville's neck and he was cut off in mid-growl. His tongue popped out and his eyes bulged.

'Hey! You're hurting him!' Sandy shouted at Squirm.

But Squirm was taking no notice. He had seen something that nobody else had seen. Behind Grazzo a sleeping giant was starting to move.

'Now tie the Glass Eyes, the Red Hair and the Other One,' Grazzo ordered. 'And be most quick before the Sausage-Eating Idiot comes back to life.'

Behind Grazzo the Sausage-Eating Idiot was already coming back to life. He was sitting up and rubbing his head.

Squirm tried to speak. But he seemed to have lost control of his tongue. All he could do was point feebly in Grazzo's direction.

'Squirm, you ant-brain,' Grazzo roared. 'Be doing what I am saying. Or you will also be the Zaldir's breakfast.'

By now Gopula was on his feet. He was not a happy giant. He looked like a giant who'd lost a sausage and found a boiled turnip.

'But Grazzo!' Squirm was shaking. His knees were knocking. And his teeth were tap-dancing round his mouth.

Grazzo looked at him in amazement.

'No buts, Squirm,' he growled. 'Do the tying up. Then we will be chucking the Sausage Eater into the mincey-mincey machine. See how he likes being the giant sausage.'

'He wouldn't like it,' said an angry voice from somewhere above Grazzo's head. 'And neither will you!'

Grazzo's eyes grew to the size of saucers. His skin looked as though it had frosted over. And his legs turned to rubber.

Gopula grabbed him by the scruff of the neck. Then he bent forward and whispered in Grazzo's ear. 'I spy with my great big eye something beginning with S.'

'Sausages?'

'How did you guess?' Gopula grinned. But the grin didn't last for long. Grazzo's teeth bit into the Giant's nose. A roar of pain filled the room. And the struggle began.

Grazzo was tiny beside the giant but he knew how to fight dirty. He kicked, scratched, bit and pulled faces.

But no matter how dirty Grazzo fought, or what hideous faces he pulled, Gopula was too strong. Slowly but surely he pushed Grazzo back until finally they were struggling right on the edge of the mincing machine pit.

Grazzo was desperate. 'Squirm!' he yelled out. 'Help!'

All this time Squirm had been frozen with fear. But the sound of his master's voice brought him back to his senses.

He hurled himself at Gopula's legs.

'I have him, Grazzo,' he shouted out. 'Just one good push and – '

Squirm pushed. Gopula overbalanced. Grazzo missed his footing. And all three crashed down into the mincing machine.

Sandy, Billy, Brains and Grenville couldn't believe their luck. For a moment they stood open-mouthed. Then Brains shouted out, 'Let's get out of here.'

That did it. Sandy, Billy and Brains raced for the door. But Grenville stayed behind. He stood barking at a switch on the wall.

'Dopey dog!' shouted Billy. 'Come on!'

Grenville just carried on barking at the switch.

Then Sandy realised. It was the mincing machine switch. She flicked the switch. The mincing machine burst into life.

Sandy shrugged her shoulders. 'They'll probably get out,' she said. 'But it'll give them something to worry about.' And with that Sandy, Billy, Brains and Grenville made their escape.

'Land of Sorcerers here we come,' yelled Billy as they headed off down the hill away from Doom Castle.

He was wrong again. They were running in the wrong direction.

'We're getting nowhere fast,' said Brains an hour later.

Brains was right. They were in the middle of Nowhere. There was nothing in every direction. No trees. No roads. No farms. No villages. Nothing. Just miles and miles of Nowhere.

'I think we're lost,' said Sandy.

'Better to be lost than found,' said Billy.

That was true. At least they were safe. Safe from Grazzo and Squirm. And Gopula. And Thugs. And Villagers. And everybody else in the Land of Badlidrempt who was looking for them.

'We can't stay here for ever though,' said Sandy. 'We've got to find the Land of Sorcerers. To get the IDT bike back off Canticle.'

'But which way is it?' said Billy.

'Grenville thinks it's this way,' said Brains.

They went the other way.

Two hours later they were still in the middle of Nowhere. And it was starting to rain.

'We're going to get soaked,' said Billy.

'Don't be silly, Billy,' Sandy laughed. 'It's been sunny everyday. This won't last.'

They looked up at the sky. Huge black clouds

were rolling in. The next thing they knew the skies had opened and rain was lashing down. Grenville turned and ran for shelter with Billy, Sandy and Brains hot on his trail. The problem was – there was no shelter.

Ten minutes later Grenville saw a bush in the distance. It wasn't a big bush. It wasn't even a medium sized bush. It was a very small bush. But it was better than no bush at all.

They dived underneath it. The rain was still lashing down.

'It's getting light over there,' said Sandy. 'It's only a shower.'

Grenville curled up in a ball, covered his eyes with his ears and went to sleep. He might only be a dog but he knew a shower when he saw one. And this wasn't one.

Grenville was right. It rained all night. It was still raining the next morning when he lifted one ear and looked out.

'It's definitely getting lighter over there,' Sandy yawned.

It wasn't. Grenville went back to sleep.

It rained all day. And all the next night.

Then it stopped. And the sun came out.

Billy, Sandy, Brains and Grenville dragged themselves out from underneath the bush.

If you've ever sat under a bush in the rain for one day and two nights, you'll know that you get three things. Very stiff. Very wet. And very hungry.

'If I don't get something to eat soon, I'll disappear,' said Billy.

'You?' said Brains. 'If you had nothing to eat for the next fifty years you still wouldn't disappear. You're so fat.'

'I'm not fat,' said Billy angrily. 'Just small for my weight.'

'Don't argue,' said Sandy. 'We're all hungry. Let's look for somewhere to eat.'

'Where?' said Billy. 'We're in the middle of Nowhere. Remember?'

Sandy remembered. There wasn't much chance of finding a café there. Then she noticed Grenville.

His nose was up. He was sniffing the air. Suddenly his tail went out. And he was off at top speed.

'Follow that Grenville!' shouted Brains.

'Why?' said Billy. 'He's never found anything yet.'

'But this time he's hungry. And that works wonders for his sense of smell,' Brains yelled back over his shoulder.

'What are we waiting for?' said Sandy. But Billy had already gone. A moment later so had Sandy.

Grenville's nose led the way across the miles and miles of nothing. Until it came to something.

The something it came to was a long low wooden cabin. Outside the long low wooden cabin was a long low wooden sign. With long low wooden letters.

'Dill and Chervil's Long Low Wooden Eating House.'

The door to the Eating House opened and a head poked out. It was a large head with stiff white hair and a bushy black beard. 'And what do you lot want then?' the head said.

'Food!' said Billy.

'Oh yes? And have you so much as booked a table?' the head asked.

'No!' said Billy.

The head nodded. 'Come in then. We never serve anybody that's booked. Do we, Chervil?'

A voice from inside shouted out, 'What was that?' But it was drowned out by the sound of footsteps rushing to get inside. Dill and Chervil had four very hungry customers.

They were the only customers. Inside the

long low wooden building there were long low wooden tables and long low wooden benches. All of them were empty.

The large white-haired head with the black beard was attached to a large black suited body with a white shirt.

'Are you Dill?' Billy asked.

'Yes. But you can call me Dill,' said Dill. 'Now what would you like?'

'A table for four, please,' said Sandy.

'Just as you like,' said Dill. 'How d'you want it cooked?'

'How do we want what cooked?'

'The table for four. Do you want it boiled? Roast with gravy? Or fried with wood chips?'

'You can't cook a table,' said Billy.

'In that case,' said Dill. 'Have it raw with a nice armchair salad.'

'Don't be dopey!' said Billy.

'They're very good value,' said Dill. 'You could have a leg each.'

'No,' said Brains. 'Nobody eats wood.'

'Woodworm do,' Dill pointed out.

'But we're not woodworm, are we?' said Sandy.

'How should I know?' Dill shrugged. 'I've never seen you before.'

'Well we're not!' yelled Billy.

'Now hurry up,' said Brains. 'I'm so hungry I could eat a horse.'

'Right,' said Dill. He turned to the kitchen. 'Chervil! One horse! And make sure it's well cooked.'

'But I don't want a horse!' Brains croaked.

'You just said you did,' said Dill.

'I didn't mean that.'

'I tell you what,' said Dill. 'Just read the menu.'

Brains read the menu. 'Raw tentacle of octosquid. Battered berries and seaweed. Boiled Bungaboyne's tusk. Gringlenurd in the hole. Fried Drewett's eggs – '

'That sounds better,' said Sandy.

'In curdled custard,' Brains continued.

'Uuurrggh!' said Sandy.

'Passion fruit surprise!'

'We'll have that!' said Sandy and Billy. Grenville licked his lips.

'It's really Boiled Bungaboyne's tusk,' Dill admitted. 'That's the surprise!'

'What else is there?' sighed Sandy.

'There's stewed Linklarter with griddled Brindletap clippings.'

'What's that like?' asked Billy.

'Revolting!' said Dill.

'Then why sell it?'

'We don't,' Dill told them. 'We give it away.'

Brains threw the menu down. 'It all sounds horrible to me.'

'It is,' Dill agreed.

'Then why not cook good things?' said Sandy. 'Like fish and chips. Or curry and rice. Or jam sponge and custard?'

Dill looked horrified. 'What? And spend all day cooking?'

'I thought that's what you did in a café?' said Brains.

Dill shook his head. 'Not in this café we don't.'

Sandy sniffed. 'But I can smell food.'

'That's Essence of Good Grub,' said Dill proudly. 'Comes in a spray can. Spray it about and you get the smell of food.'

'So how do we get some proper food round here?' asked Brains.

'Cook it yourself,' said Dill. He pointed towards the back. 'The kitchen's out there. And cook some for me and Chervil as well. We're starving!'

'Right!' said Sandy. 'We will.'

And they did.

For once Dill and Chervil's kitchen was filled

with the sounds and smells of cooking. Billy, Sandy and Brains cooked anything that wasn't moving. And one or two things that were. Grenville helped out by tasting everything he could get his lips around.

When the feast was ready it was piled onto one of the long low wooden tables and eaten. The feast not the table.

'Now that's what I call good grub, eh Chervil?' said Dill.

'Good grub! What was that?' said Chervil as he left to start the washing up.

'His hearing's not been the same since Grazzo hung him upside down inside a bell and struck midnight,' Dill whispered.

'Grazzo!'

'Not a friend of yours, is he?' Dill was looking worried.

'Definitely not!' said Brains. 'He's our biggest enemy!'

Dill looked even more worried. 'That's bad news,' he said. 'Grazzo was our enemy once. And look what happened to us.'

'What did happen to you?' asked Sandy.

Dill told them.

'Did you ever hear of Dill and Chervil's Friendly Circus?'

'You were in a circus?'

'We were the Circus! We did everything ourselves. We were the clowns. Jugglers. Tightrope walkers. Animal trainers. The lot.'

'What happened?'

'Grazzo closed down every fair and circus in the land. Except his own. We tried to carry on. That's when he got nasty.'

Dill shivered as he remembered that time.

'He said if he ever saw us again he'd throw us in with the Poison Fanged Skull Muncher. That's why we came out here. To the middle of Nowhere.'

Dill stood up and stretched. 'You better keep away from him as well.'

'We're trying to,' said Sandy. 'We're looking for the Land of Sorcerers.'

'You're in luck,' Dill smiled. 'I can show you which way to go. It's not far from here.'

'But I thought we were in the middle of Nowhere,' said Brains.

'We are,' said Dill. 'But that's right next to Somewhere. And from there it's only two days walk to the Mountains of Gloom, Grief and Woe. The Land of Sorcerers is on the other side. We'll set off as soon as we've finished eating.'

'We have finished eating,' said Brains.

'You better cook something else before you go,' said Dill. 'Might be a long time before we eat again. Isn't that right, Chervil?'

'A long time,' shouted Chervil from the kitchen. 'What was that?'

The next morning, Dill showed Billy, Sandy, Brains and Grenville the way to Somewhere. They got there in no time at all.

Somewhere looked very much like Nowhere. Except there was less of it. In the far distance were the snow-capped peaks of a range of mountains.

'The Mountains of Gloom, Grief and Woe,' Dill told them. 'The Land of Sorcerers is on the other side.'

'Why are they called the Mountains of Gloom, Grief and Woe?' Sandy asked.

'You'll find out,' said Dill, as he waved good-bye.

Sandy wished she hadn't asked.

The journey through Somewhere to the Mountains of Gloom, Grief and Woe was too easy for words. Almost nothing happened that was worth writing about. Grenville got into a fight with a cactus – he lost. Sandy couldn't find her handkerchief – it was lost. Billy argued with Brains about the best way to get cactus spikes out of a dog's nose – he told him to get lost.

By the morning of the third day the mountains were rising up in front of them. Sandy, Billy and Grenville looked at them in wonder.

'They're too high!' said Billy. 'We'll never get over them.'

But Brains was already planning a route.

'There's a valley between the two peaks,' he pointed out. 'That's the best way.'

But when they reached the entrance to the valley they stopped.

There. On a huge rock. Someone had painted the words. 'The Valley of Song and Stone. If you value your life, KEEP OUT!' Signed SALAZAR.

# Chapter 12

—

Billy turned round. And walked away. 'I'm not going down there,' he said.

'Woah! Woah!' Grenville agreed. He began to follow Billy but Brains pulled him back.

'Don't take any notice of that,' he said. 'That's just there to frighten people.'

'It works,' said Billy. 'It's frightened me.'

'Does it frighten you as much as staying in Badlidrempt for ever?' asked Sandy.

Billy stopped walking.

'If we don't get to the Land of Sorcerers we'll have to stay here. And never go home again.'

There were tears in Sandy's eyes. There were tears in Brains's and Billy's eyes as well. There weren't any tears in Grenville's eyes. They were already rolling down his face. He sat on his tail and howled.

They all sat and howled. For the first time they realised that they might never get back home.

They had to find Canticle. And that meant getting to the Land of Sorcerers whatever the risk.

Billy dried his eyes on Grenville's ear and stood up. 'Come on,' he said bravely. 'We're going through this Valley.' He pushed Grenville forward. 'You go first. Just in case.'

Grenville went first. He led the way down the Valley like a dog leading his army into battle. Or at least, like a very frightened dog leading three very frightened cowards into battle.

They had not gone far when they saw the first stone statue. Soon there were others. Frozen stiff. With looks of surprise, shock and horror on their faces.

'This is weird,' Sandy shivered. 'It's almost as if they're alive.'

'Or as if they used to be alive,' said Brains.

'Spooky!' said Billy.

Grenville stopped. He'd spotted something else. Someone was walking down the Valley towards them. It was Salazar.

'Hide!' said Billy.

But it was too late. Salazar had already seen them. He waved a greeting. First with one hand. Then with the other hand. Then with both hands.

'He seems friendly enough,' said Sandy. 'He keeps smiling at us.'

'So does a Crocodile before it eats you,' said Billy.

Salazar had long curly hair, held in place by a purple and orange headband. He was wearing sandals with no socks. Lime-green flared trousers. A yellow tee shirt with pink flowers on it. And a furry waistcoat.

'Funny clothes!' Brains murmured.

'What do you mean?' said Sandy. 'Our Granddad wears clothes like that.'

By now they could hear that Salazar was singing. A happy sort of song. With very strange words.

Singing along
In the Valley of Song
Trying to trick and catch you.
If you don't sing
Then the magic will work
And turn you into a statue.
Then you will stay here everyday
Never move on or go away.
Frozen quite still
In the shade of the hill.

Oh tell me will
You stay?

Sing me the song
Sing it loud and strong.
Sing me the song
Sing it loud and strong.

'Hi, man!' Salazar smiled. 'Salazar's the name.
Sure is good to see you. I just love visitors.'

Salazar shook Sandy, Billy and Brains by the
hand. He shook Grenville by the tail.

'That's the wrong end,' said Brains.

'What's the wrong end between friends?'
smiled Salazar.

Grenville sneaked off to sulk in the shade of
a rock.

'Say,' said Salazar. 'We are friends, aren't we?'

'Of course,' said Sandy.

'Definitely!' said Brains.

'Yep,' said Billy.

'Grrrrr!' growled Grenville.

Salazar's smile disappeared.

'That's just his way of being friendly,' said
Sandy.

The smile came back. 'That's OK then. We're

all friends together. For now and for ever.'

Grenville growled again. He didn't like the way Salazar said 'for ever'.

'That sure is one friendly cat,' said Salazar.

'He's not a cat. He's a dog,' said Sandy quickly. She could see that Grenville was sharpening his teeth and they needed Salazar's help. 'Is this the way to the Land of Sorcerers?' she asked.

'Sure is!'

Sandy, Billy and Brains breathed three sighs of relief. Grenville didn't. He knew that something was wrong. He was right.

'Better hurry then,' said Sandy.

Salazar frowned. 'Hey, man!' he said. 'You ain't going nowhere.'

'Why not?' said Billy.

'This is the Valley of Song and Stone,' said Salazar. 'Nobody leaves here. Not once they come to visit.'

'Why not?' said Sandy. 'You said you like visitors.'

'I love visitors. I love them so much I never let them leave.'

Brains gulped. 'What do you mean? You never let them leave?'

Salazar pointed at the statues. 'Here they are, man. Still visiting. For now and for ever.'

'But these are statues,' said Billy. 'Not people.'

'They're statues now,' Salazar agreed. 'But when they came here they were just as live as you and me.'

'Then what turned them into stone?' Sandy could hardly get the words out.

'Magic,' Salazar grinned. 'The same magic that will turn you into stone. Unless you win.'

'Win what?'

'The singing contest.'

'What singing contest?'

'Everybody who comes into the Valley of Song and Stone has to take part in the contest. Against me. The one who sings longest wins. The other turns to stone.' Salazar looked proudly round at the statues. 'Ain't nobody beat me yet.'

'What happens if we don't take part?' Brains gulped.

'You turn to stone anyway.'

Sandy, Billy, Brains and Grenville felt as though they'd already turned to stone. They were frozen with fear.

'Ready to start?' asked Salazar.

'But we don't know the song,' Sandy blurted out.

'That's OK, man. First I sing the song. Then

you sing it. Then me. Then you. On and on till one of us can't sing no more.'

Salazar started to sing. The same song that he had sung earlier.

Sandy, Billy, and Brains had never learnt a song so quickly. The moment Salazar finished singing they started. When they stopped singing Salazar started. And so it carried on.

And on. And on.

All afternoon. Into the evening. And then on into the dark of the night. Over and over again the song was sung. First by Salazar. Then by Sandy, Billy and Brains.

They had never sung so much before. But now they were singing for their lives.

Verse after verse. Chorus after chorus. Their voices rang out. On and endlessly on. Until the sun began to rise. They had sung all night. But now as dawn broke, so did their voices.

The strain was too much. They simply couldn't carry on. First Brains's voice gave out. Then Billy started to croak.

Finally only Sandy could sing. But for how long?

'Keep going, Sandy,' Billy croaked. 'You've got to. Or we'll turn to stone.'

Salazar's voice sounded as though he could

carry on for ever.

'It's no good,' Sandy whispered. 'My throat's like sandpaper. I think we've had it.'

'Sing me the song
Sing it loud and strong,'
sang Salazar.
'Sing me the song,
Sing it loud and strong.'
Salazar's turn was over.

Sandy opened her mouth. But no sound came out. Her voice had gone. She looked hopefully at Brains and Billy but they were silent. It looked as though the contest was well and truly over.

# Chapter 13

—

Sandy, Billy and Brains couldn't believe their ears. A new voice was singing.

'Arrrroooohhh! Rooohhhh! Rooohhhh! Rooohhhh! Rooooh! Roooh! Rooooooooooh! Roorooooohhh!'

The tune was shaky. The words weren't clear. But the song was being sung. Grenville had taken over.

'Hey, man!' Salazar protested. 'What's this cat doing?'

'He's singing,' croaked Brains.

'Singing!' bellowed Salazar. 'That ain't singing. That's howling. And this is a singing contest. Not a howling contest.'

'But that's how he sings!'

Grenville was coming to the end of the song.

'Man, if he sings like that, he is a lousy

singer. And this contest is well and truly – '

But Salazar never finished the sentence. His mouth stopped moving. His skin turned grey. His body froze. His eyes went blank. In a split second he had turned to stone.

Grenville had finished singing. And Salazar had failed to start. The contest was over. Billy, Sandy and Brains had won. Thanks to Grenville.

Billy, Sandy and Brains gave three hearty croaks. Then sank to the ground exhausted. Within seconds they were asleep. Grenville glared at them. So that was all the thanks he got! Still, he was feeling very pleased with himself. He'd never realised he was such a good singer.

He took a deep breath and howled the first line of the song. A rock hit him on the head.

'Belt up, Grenville!' croaked Billy. 'We're trying to get some kip here.'

Grenville curled up and closed his eyes. He was pretty tired himself.

When Sandy woke it was night again.

In the starlight she could just make out the outlines of the frozen statues. There was nothing else to see.

Except the single pair of eyes peeping out from behind one of the figures. Sandy looked away.

Eyes!

Sandy looked back. The eyes had gone. Then they appeared again. Nearer this time.

Sandy kicked the others awake.

'What's the matter?' Brains snapped. He was always bad-tempered when woken by a boot in the back.

'Look!' Sandy whispered. 'There's somebody watching us.'

Brains, Billy and Grenville looked.

'It's just a statue,' Billy scoffed.

'Statues' eyes don't move.'

The eyes moved.

'Could be a trick of the light,' Brains gulped.

'There isn't any light!'

'A trick of the dark then!'

The eyes moved again.

Then Sandy, Billy, Brains and Grenville moved.

In a blind panic they raced along the valley. But there were statues everywhere. They kept bumping into them. It was like trying to find your way through a wood. In the dark. Wearing a blindfold. And with a bucket over your head.

Finally, Billy stopped. 'This is hopeless,' he moaned. 'I keep bumping into statues.'

Sandy screamed.

'What's wrong?' asked Brains.

'The statue I just bumped into. It moved!'

'No it didn't,' said a voice.

Silence! Everyone was afraid to speak.

Sandy took a deep breath. 'Who said that?'

'Nobody!' the voice replied.

'Yes they did,' said Sandy. 'Was it you, Billy?'

'No.'

'Brains?'

'Not me.'

'And it definitely wasn't Grenville,' said Sandy.

'Yes it was,' said the voice.

'No it wasn't!' said Sandy, Billy, Brains and Grenville.

'Well it wasn't me.' said the voice.

'Yes it was,' said Sandy, Billy, Brains and Grenville.

'All right, I give up,' said the voice. 'It was me.'

It was an odd voice. With a strange crowing sound to it. But it wasn't a cruel voice.

'Who are you?' Sandy asked.

'I'm Zeti! The Abominable Crowman!'

'Don't you mean Abominable Snowman?' said Brains.

'No,' said Zeti. 'I'm a crowman. Part man. Part crow.'

'You must look pretty weird,' said Billy.

Zeti started to cry. 'Of caw–se I do,' he sobbed. 'I look aw-ful. Just one look and people run away. That's why I only come out at night. When nobody can see me.'

Billy felt terrible. He hadn't meant to upset Zeti. But the Abominable Crowman was breaking his heart.

'See what you've done, Billy,' Sandy snapped. She wanted to reach out and comfort the poor Crowman. But it was pitch black and she wasn't sure where he was. 'Don't cry,' she told him. 'I'm sure you don't look that bad.'

'No,' said Brains. 'And anyway, you shouldn't hide just because you look different. Be brave. And come out in the daylight.'

'I couldn't,' Zeti snuffled. 'If I did, I'd get caw-t.'

'Caught?' said Brains. 'Who by?'

'By Grazzo and Squirm, of caw-se. They want to put me in their Circus,' Zeti sobbed. 'That's why I stay up the mountain all day. They can't catch me there. I only come down here at night.

To see the statues. They're my only friends. I taw-k to them.'

Everybody was so upset by Zeti's sad tale that it was a few minutes before anybody could speak. Then Brains started to tell Zeti about their battles with Grazzo and Squirm.

Zeti hadn't enjoyed himself so much for years. Especially the bits about Grazzo and Squirm being chased by the Zaldir. And falling in the mincing machine.

'I wish there was something I could do to help you get back home,' Zeti said after Brains had finished the story.

'Perhaps there is,' said Sandy. 'Do you know a way over the mountains to the Land of Sorcerers?'

'Of caw-se, I do,' said Zeti. 'I know these mountains like the back of my wing.'

'Then take us there.'

Zeti thought for a moment. 'There's a problem,' he said. 'I could only do it in daylight.'

'What's wrong with that?' asked Brains.

'Be-caw-se then you'll see me. And you'll run away. People aw-lways do.' There was a terrible sadness in his voice again.

Sandy spoke for everybody when she said, 'We won't run away. Honest!'

'Hmmmm!' said Zeti. 'We'll see what happens when the sun comes up.'

When the sun rose over the Valley of Song and Stone, Zeti hid behind a statue. But Sandy took him by the wing and led him out into the open.

Part man, part crow, Zeti was the strangest creature Sandy, Billy, Brains and Grenville had ever seen.

'I can see why people run off when they see him,' Billy whispered to Brains.

But Brains tried not to show it. 'I don't know what all the fuss is about,' he told Zeti.

'Nor me,' said Sandy.

'Woah! Woah!' Grenville agreed.

Zeti pointed at Billy. 'What about him?' he said. 'What does he think?'

Billy gulped. Then took a deep breath. 'You're the best looking Abominable Crowman I've ever seen,' he said.

Zeti grinned. At least, they thought he grinned. It's difficult to tell when somebody has a beak instead of a mouth. But there was a smile in his eyes as he led the way up the mountainside.

'Billy, you just made an Abominable Crowman very happy,' said Sandy.

Keeping up with Zeti was not easy. Before long Sandy, Billy, Brains and Grenville had to rest. But the Crowman seemed to think that they were still behind him.

'Shout!' Billy gasped. 'Tell him to wait.'

'No!' warned Brains. 'No shouting. Not on a mountain. You could start a landslide. And anyway he'll stop soon.' Brains was right. A few more bounding leaps and Zeti turned and looked back.

Sandy waved. But instead of waving back, Zeti flapped his wings and hopped from foot to foot. Something had upset him.

'Wonder what's wrong?' Sandy wondered.

The next moment they found out. Zeti opened his beak and yelled at the top of his voice, 'Caw-tion!'

The single word echoed down the rocky mountainside.

'What's he mean caution?' said Billy.

'I don't know,' said Brains. 'But if he yells like that he'll bring the rocks down on us.'

Zeti did yell. Even louder. 'Behind you!' he roared.

A scattering of loose stones started to roll down the slope. Gathering speed as they went, they set bigger rocks moving.

'He must be crazy,' said Brains. 'He's starting a landslide.'

But Sandy had turned to look behind. What she saw explained everything. A mad Horde was rushing up the mountain towards them. A horde led by Grazzo, Squirm and Gopula.

'Come on,' shouted Sandy. 'Let's go.'

There was only one way to go. Up. Up the mountain. Away from Grazzo, Squirm and Gopula.

But coming down the mountain was a landslide!

What had started as a few loose stones and chippings was growing bigger all the time. Soon it seemed that half the mountain was crashing down. And it was heading straight for them.

Below, the mad Hordes were scattering in all directions. Racing to get out of the way.

'Dive for cover!' yelled Brains.

The only protection was a few scrubby bushes.

They dived behind them. But it was no good. It was like trying to stop a bulldozer with a feather. The landslide slammed into the bushes.

The next moment the bushes, Sandy, Billy,

Brains and Grenville were tumbling down the mountainside in a flurry of dust, stones and rocks.

# Chapter 14

—

The landslide came to rest far below in the Valley of Song and Stone. There was an eerie silence. The dust settled. Nothing moved.

Then one by one Sandy, Billy, Brains and Grenville picked themselves up and looked around.

It was a miracle they were still alive. But they were. Sandy and Billy had some cuts and bruises. Brains had cracked his glasses. And Grenville's left ear was never the same again. But they were alive. And that wasn't all. The landslide had left Grazzo and the Horde stranded halfway up the mountain.

Billy, Sandy, Brains and Grenville had escaped again. They should have been over-joyed. But they weren't. They knew that their best chance of getting to the Land of Sorcerers had gone.

'Rats!' yelled Billy. He turned round and kicked the side of the mountain.

A hollow thud echoed round the valley.

'Sounds hollow,' said Brains.

It was.

How do I know? Because a slab of rock creaked open and a little man stepped out.

'I am not the Keeper of the Door and my name is not Chadregar,' he announced.

'Sorry?' said Sandy.

'I am not the Keeper of the Door and my name is not Chadregar,' the little man repeated.

'Didn't say it was,' said Billy.

'Yes, you did.'

'No I didn't.'

'I didn't say you did,' the little man argued.

'Yes you did.'

'No I didn't.'

'Stop!' said Sandy. There was something funny going on. But she wasn't sure what. She tried a question. 'Where's the Land of Sorcerers?'

'Don't know. Never heard of it,' the little man replied.

'You've never heard of the Land of Sorcerers!' said Sandy.

'Yes, I have,' the little man snapped.

'Can you tell us the way then?'

'It's not through this secret passage,' the little man insisted.

Suddenly Brains realised what was happening. 'I've met people like this before,' he whispered.

'So have I,' said Billy. 'They're called nutters.'

'No, it's a kind of illness,' said Brains. 'They just can't tell the truth. They always have to argue. To say the opposite of whatever you say.'

'Is there a cure for it?' asked Sandy.

'Yes,' said Billy. 'A punch on the nose.'

'Leave this to me, William,' said Brains. 'I think I know how to deal with him.'

Brains turned to the little man.

'Excuse me,' he said. 'Your name isn't Chadregar, is it?'

'Yes, it is,' said Chadregar.

It was working. Brains winked at Sandy, Billy and Grenville.

Grenville winked back. There was something in his eye.

Brains turned to Chadregar again. 'There isn't a secret passage through the mountain that leads to the Land of Sorcerers, is there?'

'Yes, there is,' Chadregar insisted. 'It's this way.' He led the way into the tunnel.

Brains followed him. 'Land of Sorcerers here we come!' he said.

Sandy, Billy and Grenville stepped inside. Chadregar pushed the slab of rock shut.

'Crikey! It's dark in here,' said Billy. 'I can hardly see my hand in front of my face.'

'Yes, you can,' said Chadregar. 'Don't follow me,' he added.

They followed him.

The inside of the mountain was a maze of tunnels. Yet Chadregar seemed to know exactly which way to go.

Deeper and deeper into the mountain he led them. Turning left, then right, then right again, then straight ahead.

And still they carried on. Brains first, then Sandy, then Billy and last of all –

'Just a minute!' said Brains. 'I shouldn't be in the lead. What's happened to Chadregar?'

Chadregar had gone. Disappeared. Vanished. Done a runner. Left them in the lurch. However you said it the result was the same. They were up a dark tunnel without a guide.

'Perhaps we just took a wrong turn,' suggested Sandy.

'Perhaps,' said Brains.

So they called out. Yelled for help. Shouted

Chadregar's name. Yoo-hooed until they were blue in the face.

Nothing. Chadregar had fooled them.

'I said a punch on the nose was the only cure,' said Billy.

'Ruff, ruff!' Grenville agreed. Though he was thinking a bite on the backside would have worked just as well.

But it was too late for that. They were on their own in the middle of a mountain. They couldn't stay where they were. So they went on.

Through tunnel after tunnel. Twisting and turning. Going up, going down. Not knowing where they were. Getting nowhere. Until –

Grenville heard a sound.

A tiny noise in the distance. So tiny that only Grenville could hear it. His ears were up like satellite dishes. He set off towards the noise. His ears twitching. Each tunnel taking him closer to the sound. The sound which was getting louder all the time. Finally even Brains, Billy and Sandy could hear it.

It was a voice. Someone was moaning.

Grenville scuttled on. Through the darkness. Until finally there was a light. A dim, flickering light coming from a cave. Grenville stopped. So did Sandy, Brains and Billy.

'What do you think?' whispered Sandy.

'Could be Chadregar,' Brains murmured.

'Or Grazzo!' Billy hissed.

Sandy pushed Billy forward. 'Go and find out.'

'Why me?' breathed Billy.

'Do it!'

Billy did it. He tiptoed towards the light. He paused. Then peered round the corner.

There was a sudden explosion of sound as Billy yelled, 'Canticle!'

Brains, Sandy and Grenville raced forward.

There, huddled in a corner of the cave – a stub of candle flickering at his feet – sat Canticle.

Canticle the Wizard. Canticle the enemy of Grazzo and Squirm. Canticle the moaner in the dark. Canticle the stealer of IDT bikes!

He looked lonely and unhappy. Tired and hungry. Cold and scared. But most of all he looked captured. The Wizard's hands and feet were tied. And his mouth was gagged.

He hardly had the strength to moan.

'Untie him!'

Billy and Brains attacked the knotted ropes. Sandy took off the gag.

Canticle gasped for breath. 'What are you

doing here?' he said wearily. He didn't seem too excited about being set free.

'Looking for you,' said Sandy. 'You stole our bike.'

'And we can't get home without it,' Brains told him.

Canticle looked at Brains. 'You must be the Glass Eyes,' he said. 'I heard Grazzo and Squirm talking about you.'

'When?' said Brains.

'Earlier,' Canticle sighed. 'Just before they went looking for you.'

'Looking for us?' said Sandy. 'Where are they now?'

'Right behind you, Red Hair,' said a voice from right behind them.

Sandy, Billy, Brains and Grenville twisted round. They knew what they were going to see. And they saw it. Grazzo and Squirm. As evil as ever.

They'd walked straight into their trap. It was the end of the journey. There was no way home.

# Chapter 15

—

Grazzo glowed with delight. His eyes gleamed with pleasure. His grin was as wide as a very wide grin.

'So my friends, you are in my power once more again. And this time there will be no escaping.'

'That's what you think!' said Brains. It was what Brains thought as well but he didn't want Grazzo to know that.

Grazzo roared with laughter. 'Most funny, Glass Eyes. Is it not, Squirm?'

Squirm began to cackle madly. 'Oh yes, Grazzo. It is the most biggest joke that I am hearing since – '

'Squirm!' Grazzo snapped.

'Yes, Grazzo?'

'Shut up and be listening.'

'Yes, Grazzo.'

Squirm shut up and listened as Grazzo gave his orders.

'You be staying here. While I am bringing the Sausage Giant and the Chadregar to help us.'

Squirm's jaw dropped. 'But Grazzo,' he whined. 'Do not be leaving me here with the Hairy Creature.'

'Lily-livered daisy!'

Grazzo grabbed Squirm by the neck and shook him till his face turned purple.

'What danger can the Hairy Creature be?'

Grenville growled and showed his teeth.

But Grazzo was ready for this. From under his coat he pulled out a treble-barrelled shotgun. He pointed it at Grenville's head.

Grenville stopped growling and wagged his tail. He knew when he was beaten.

Grazzo handed the gun to Squirm, gave him one final shake and stumped off down the tunnel.

'It's a good job you're his friend,' Brains told Squirm. 'Or he might be really nasty to you.'

'Silence!' shouted Squirm. 'Do not say these things about the Great Grazzo.'

'Why not? What will you do?' asked Billy.

Squirm tried to think of something really horrible. 'I will shout very loud. And pull scary faces. Like this.'

Squirm pulled a scary face. Not even Canticle was scared. Billy, Sandy and Brains just laughed. And Grenville lay on his back and kicked his legs in the air.

'Shut up!' Squirm yelled. 'Or I bang-bang-bang with the three-holed banger.'

The words were odd but everybody knew what Squirm meant. Shut up or he'd shoot.

But would he do it? There was only one way to find out. And nobody wanted to be the first to try it.

One thing was obvious. They had to escape before Grazzo, Gopula and Chadregar arrived.

Sandy inched towards Brains and Billy. 'What are we going to do?' she whispered.

'No talking,' shouted Squirm. 'It is not to be allowed. One more word and the firestick explodes.'

It was then that Brains had an idea.

'What about singing?' he asked.

Squirm looked at him as though he'd gone mad.

So did Sandy, Billy and Grenville. Even Canticle was a bit surprised.

'Well?' said Brains.

Squirm was puzzled. 'I no understand the question.'

'It's simple,' said Brains. 'We aren't allowed to talk. But can we sing?'

'Sing?' Squirm repeated. 'No. No talking. No singing. Nothing.'

'That's a pity,' sighed Brains. 'Because Grenville is a wonderful singer.'

Squirm was amazed.

So was Grenville.

'The Hairy Creature sings?' asked Squirm.

'Like a...' Brains couldn't think of the best description.

'Bird!' said Sandy.

'Dog!' said Billy.

'Like a bird-dog,' said Brains. 'Of course, he can't sing now. Because you said no singing! And we always do what you say.'

'You do?' said Squirm.

'Oh, yes,' Brains told him. 'Because you're so scary when you're angry.'

Squirm was overjoyed. Nobody had ever told him he was scary before. It was Grazzo that people were frightened of, not him. In fact, Squirm was as frightened of Grazzo as everybody else was. And no matter how hard he tried he could never be as nasty and evil as Grazzo. Sometimes Squirm wasn't even sure that he wanted to be nasty and evil.

But he never told anybody that. Especially not Grazzo.

Still, it was good to know that somebody was scared of him. He pointed at Grenville. 'Hairy Creature!' he ordered. 'Be singing.'

Grenville still didn't know what Brains was up to but he sang anyway.

Nobody was really sure what the song was. Brains thought it was 'How Much Is That Doggy In The Window?' Billy thought it was 'You Ain't Nothing But A Hound Dog.' Sandy was pretty sure it was 'And They Called It Puppy Love.' Canticle had an idea Grenville was still warming up. And Squirm thought that whatever song it was, Grenville must be singing it backwards.

They were all wrong. Grenville was singing the song that Salazar had sung in the Valley of Song and Stone. And he was singing it loud and strong. So loud and strong that Squirm had to shove his fingers in his ears.

'Now we can talk without him hearing us,' Brains hissed. 'We've got to get away while Squirm is on his own.'

'He's not on his own,' Billy pointed out. 'He's got a treble-barrelled shotgun with him.'

'That'll be no good if he can't see us,' said Brains.

Sandy and Billy looked at each other. Then they looked at Canticle.

'Can you make us invisible, Canticle?' asked Sandy.

Canticle shook his head. 'I haven't got that much magic. Not without my Magic Watch.'

'Don't worry,' said Brains. 'I can make us disappear.'

'How?' asked Sandy.

'You'll see,' Brains told her.

By now, Squirm had had enough. He took his fingers out of his ears and yelled, 'Stop, Hairy Creature!'

Grenville sang to the end of the chorus. Stopped. And took a bow. He would have done better to take a bow–wow. Nobody clapped. Especially not Squirm.

'Such horrible, horrible singing,' he groaned. 'Never have I heard such a terrible voice. And always the same words.'

'Yes,' Brains admitted. 'It was pretty awful. But we always let him have a good sing on his birthday.'

Squirm was shocked. He had no idea it was Grenville's birthday. Neither did Grenville. Nor Billy and Sandy.

'Today is the birthday of the Hairy Creature?' said Squirm.

Brains nodded. 'I'd almost forgotten,' he told

Squirm. 'We haven't even sung Happy Birthday. We'll never get a chance to sing it now.'

Tears filled Squirm's eyes. 'But that is so so sad,' he sniffed. 'Poor poor Hairy Creature.' Then Squirm had an idea. It was the idea that Brains wanted him to have.

'Should we be singing Happy Birthday to the Hairy Creature now?' Squirm suggested. 'Before the Great Grazzo comes back?'

Brains shook his head. 'It's a nice idea. But we haven't got a cake with candles to blow out. And you can't sing Happy Birthday without candles, can you, Sandy?'

Suddenly Sandy saw what Brains was planning. 'Oh no,' she said. 'You have to have at least one candle to blow out.'

It was then that Squirm had the second idea that Brains wanted him to have.

'There is no cake,' he said. 'But there is one candle.'

Squirm pointed to the candle that was flickering in the middle of the cave.

Brains gasped. Sandy clapped her hands in delight. Billy cheered. And Grenville wagged his tail like mad. Only Canticle didn't know what was going on.

'Squirm, you're a genius!' said Brains.

Squirm blushed bright red. He had never been told he was a genius before. Usually Grazzo told him that he was an idiot. But perhaps Grazzo was wrong.

Sandy, Billy, Brains and Squirm gathered round the candle to sing Happy Birthday to Grenville. Sandy grabbed hold of Canticle and pulled him into the circle.

'Come on, Canticle,' she whispered. 'You don't want to be left behind, do you?'

'Left behind?' Canticle's eyes brightened. Now Squirm was the only one who didn't know what was going on.

'Everybody ready?' said Brains.

Everybody was ready.

They began to sing.

'Happy Birthday to you.

Happy Birthday to you.

Happy Birthday, dear Grenville.

Happy Birthday to you.'

Everybody cheered.

Grenville took a deep breath and blew out the candle.

The light disappeared. So did Grenville, Brains, Billy, Sandy and Canticle.

Squirm was still cheering when he realised nobody else was. He stopped. It was dark. Very dark. It was also quiet. Very quiet. And he had a horrible feeling that he was on his own.

'Hello,' he called out. 'Is anybody there?'

There wasn't.

Everything had gone wrong. He had made a mess of things again.

'Squirm!' he said to himself. 'The Great Grazzo is right. You are not a genius. Just one idiot.'

He sat there. In the dark. With tears rolling down his cheeks.

He was still sitting there when Grazzo got back and found that Sandy, Billy, Brains, Grenville and Canticle had escaped.

I won't tell you what Grazzo said. I bet you can guess.

You bubling idiot, you let them excspape.

# Chapter 16

—

The chase was on. Sandy, Billy, Brains, Grenville and Canticle were racing for their lives through the dark tunnels. Searching desperately for the way out.

It was like looking for a tadpole in the ocean.

Sandy led the way. Then Brains led the way. Then Billy. Then Grenville. And last of all Canticle. It made no difference. Nobody knew where they were going.

It needed a miracle if they were ever going to find their way out. The miracle happened. As if by magic they saw daylight ahead.

They were back at the entrance to the Valley of Song and Stone. And the door in the rock was wide open! It was the first bit of good luck they'd had since they arrived in the Land of Badlidrempt. It was also the last.

Suddenly the light was blocked out by a shadow. The shadow of a giant. A sausage-eating giant. A sausage-eating, games-playing giant. The shadow turned into a shape. The shape turned into a body. And the body turned out to be Gopula.

'Well, if it ain't my four little sausages,' grinned the giant. 'Like to play a game with me?'

'What game?' said Billy, backing away.

'Hunt the sausages!'

'No thanks.'

'Never mind,' said Gopula. 'That game's over now. Because I've just found them.'

Gopula stepped forward but Sandy had an idea.

'I know another game we could play,' she said.

'Another game?' Gopula's eyes lit up. 'What is it?'

'Hide and seek. Want to play?'

'Oh yes!' said the giant.

'Right,' said Sandy. 'You're on first. Just close your eyes and count to one thousand.'

Gopula closed his eyes and started to count.

'One…two…three…'

By the time Gopula got to three, Sandy, Billy, Brains, Grenville and Canticle had gone. Back into the tunnels.

'Four…five…'

By the time he got to five, Gopula knew he'd been fooled.

A roar of anger raced along the passageways. Closely followed by the giant himself.

The chase was on again. Only this time they could hear the shuddering thuds of the giant's footsteps behind them. Getting closer all the time.

But something strange was happening. Billy was the first to notice it.

'Hey! I am getting bigger,' he yelled.

'Don't be stupid,' said Brains. 'It's the tunnels that are getting smaller.'

And they were. They were getting smaller all the time.

'That's OK,' shouted Sandy. 'Gopula's bigger than us. The smaller the tunnels get the more chance we've got of escaping.'

Sandy was right. Already Gopula's footsteps were slowing down. But it wasn't all good news. As they went on, the tunnel narrowed down to an opening the size of an elephant's back leg. It was barely big enough to crawl through.

'Keep going,' Sandy told them.

'I'm not sure I can,' said Canticle.

'Just get in there,' said Sandy. 'We'll push you if you get stuck.'

Canticle crawled slowly in.

'And hurry up,' shouted Billy. 'Gopula's nearly here.'

Brains dived in behind Canticle. Then Sandy and Billy. With Grenville at the back.

They were just in time. Gopula's head crashed against the rock as he tried to force his way in. But it was no use. He was too big.

'Come back!' he roared.

'No chance!' laughed Billy. 'You come and get us.'

Gopula did just that. He thrust his arm into the tunnel and grabbed hold of Grenville's tail.

'Uuuurrggh?'

Suddenly Grenville was going backwards.

'He's got Grenville!' yelled Billy. 'He's pulling him back.'

Billy grabbed Grenville's collar. Sandy grabbed Billy. Brains grabbed Sandy. And Canticle – well he just kept crawling forward. He wasn't bothered whether Gopula captured the Woolly Sausage or not. As long as he got away himself.

And so a tug of war started. Gopula was on one side. Billy, Sandy and Brains were on the the other. And Grenville was the rope.

Billy, Sandy and Brains tugged like mad. But

Gopula was winning. Slowly he was pulling Grenville back. It needed somebody brilliant to come up with an idea.

Billy wasn't brilliant. But he did have a brilliant idea. At least, he thought it was brilliant. He let go!

Sandy and Brains didn't think it was a brilliant idea. They couldn't believe what Billy had done. But before they could say anything. Billy was shouting instructions to the disappearing dog.

'Now, Grenville,' he yelled. 'Show Gopula what it's like to be a sausage.'

Grenville knew what Billy meant. He twisted round and sank his teeth into Gopula's hand. There was a scream of pain. And Gopula let go. The next moment Grenville was scrabbling back towards Billy.

'Now let's get moving,' Billy yelled.

Which would have been a good idea if there'd been anywhere to go. But there wasn't. Because in front of them Canticle was crawling back.

'You're going the wrong way,' yelled Brains as his head bashed into Canticle's rear end.

'No, I'm not,' Canticle insisted. 'They're in front of us.'

'Who are?'

'Grazzo and Squirm!'

A roar of triumph from the most evil man in Badlidrempt echoed along the tunnel. 'So, my friends, we meet again. Did I not say that no one escapes from the Great Grazzo?'

There is an old saying in the land of Badlidrempt. 'When you are stuck in the middle of a mountain, with a sausage-eating giant behind you and the Great Grazzo in front, then you're in big trouble.' It was a stupid saying. But it was very true.

There was only one thing to decide. Whether to go forward and end up fighting the Seven Headed Zaldir. Or to go back and end up in Gopula's mincing machine.

'Forward!' said Billy.

'Back!' said Brains.

Sandy sighed. 'Do you two have to argue about everything?'

'He started it,' Brains said.

'Did not!' said Billy.

'Just shut up,' Sandy told them. 'You'll be fighting next.'

And then Sandy had her brilliant idea. 'It's not us that should be fighting. It's them!'

'What are you talking about?' said Brains.

'She's flipped,' said Billy.

But she hadn't.

'Hey, Gopula,' Sandy shouted out. 'Your pals, Grazzo and Squirm, are here. And you know what they just said about you?'

'What did they say?' the giant bellowed back.

'They said you were a dopey, ropey, greedy, weedy, junky monkey of a sausage-eating nutter!'

There was a gasp. Then –

'They said what!?'

'That you'd got less brain than the back end of a worm,' Sandy continued. 'And that once you'd helped them capture us, they'd knock you out and shove you in your own mincing machine!'

A roar of anger blasted down the tunnel. Gopula was not a happy giant.

At the other end, a puzzled Grazzo heard the shout and called back. 'What is this going on down there?'

Gopula knew that Grazzo had said something. But he couldn't tell what.

Sandy helped out. 'Grazzo said, "Tighten your teeth, you old barrel of bangers, before he comes down there and turns you into a ton of chipolatas."'

Gopula was shaking with rage now. So was the tunnel.

'Not only that,' Sandy continued. 'He says they're not frightened of you. Because you couldn't even burst your way out of a sausage skin!'

That did it. Gopula's temper exploded. Using all his superhuman strength he forced his way up the narrow tunnel.

Billy panicked. 'He's going to cause an earthquake!'

Rocks were cracking. Shaking. Shuddering. Splitting. The whole mountain seemed to be moving. The next moment the roof caved in. There was an eruption of dust and stones. And then blue sky!

They were out of the mountain. But so were Grazzo and Squirm. Up the slope they were pushing their way out of the rubble.

An evil grin spread across Grazzo's face. Within seconds the grin was wiped away as a voice from lower down the mountain bellowed, 'So I couldn't burst my way out of a sausage skin, couldn't I?'

Grazzo and Squirm didn't stop to argue. They raced off up the slope with Gopula thundering after them.

'That should keep them busy for a bit,' said Sandy.

'Long enough for us to get well on our way to the Land of Sorcerers,' said Brains. And then he stopped.

Brains looked at Sandy. Sandy looked at Billy. Billy looked at Grenville. Then they all looked at Canticle.

'Something wrong?' Canticle was trying to look innocent. It just made him look shifty.

Nobody said anything. But everybody moved nearer. And they kept on moving nearer until Canticle was surrounded.

'Better hurry,' he said. 'It's a long way to the Land of Sorcerers.'

'We were only going there to find you,' said Brains.

'To get our IDT bike back,' said Sandy.

'So where is it?' said Billy.

Canticle pointed to a big red rock further up the valley. 'Behind that rock,' he told them. 'I hid it there.'

'Is this some sort of trick?' said Sandy.

'Of course not,' said Canticle. 'I'll take you to it now.'

Nobody expected the IDT bike to be there. Not even Canticle. You couldn't leave anything for ten minutes in Badlidrempt without it disappearing. But when they got to the red rock there it was.

'See?' smirked Canticle. 'I told you so.'

Brains grabbed the bike and checked it over.

Billy and Sandy held their breath. Grenville held his tail between his teeth.

Brains looked up. 'I think it's OK,' he grinned.

Sandy and Billy cheered. Grenville howled with delight and almost choked. He forgot that he still had his tail in his mouth!

'It's a bit shaky,' said Brains after Grenville had stopped coughing. 'So we better not ride here. It's too bumpy. We'll carry it to the end of the valley.'

Billy, Sandy and Brains picked up the bike but Canticle stopped them.

'Just one moment,' he said. 'You can't take that. I still need it to get back to the Land of Sorcerers. It's not safe to go over the mountain now.'

'Tough luck. You can't have it,' said Billy.

'In that case...' Canticle raised his arm in the air.

'Wait!' shouted Sandy. The last time Canticle had done that they'd gone flying. Without a plane. 'We'll take you back to the Land of Sorcerers first. Then we'll go home ourselves.'

Canticle lowered his arm.

'Don't be nutty!' Billy yelled. 'That'll take for ever. We'll probably get caught again!'

Canticle raised his arm again.

'OK!' said Billy. 'We'll do it.'

But Brains had other plans. At the end of the valley, he turned to Canticle. 'I'll just tighten up a few nuts and bolts and things. You have a rest.'

'Is this a trick?' Canticle was suspicious.

'Oh no,' Brains told him. 'You're much too clever to be tricked.'

'I suppose so,' said Canticle and he sat down with his back against a tree.

Brains began fiddling with the bike.

'What are you doing?' whispered Sandy.

'This bike will never carry all of us,' Brains hissed. 'We've got to get rid of Canticle!'

Billy gulped. 'Bump him off, you mean?'

'No, stupid!' hissed Brains. 'Just make him think about something else while we get away.'

'But how?'

Brains winked. 'Leave it to me.'

Canticle was getting jumpy. 'What are you whispering about?' he called out.

Brains stood up. 'We were having an argument,' he said. 'About how clever you are. I said you were a genius. But Billy said you were a birdbrain.'

'What!' Canticle snapped.

Billy gulped. He hoped Brains knew what he was doing. So did Brains.

'The thing is,' Brains carried on. 'I said you could solve a riddle. But Billy said you wouldn't have a clue.'

'Tell me the riddle now,' said Canticle. 'I'll soon have the answer.'

Brains smiled. His plan was working. 'All right then. What occurs once in a minute. Twice in a moment. But never in a thousand years?'

Canticle gulped. 'Hmmm! That's a hard one,' he said. 'What occurs once in a minute. Twice in a moment. But never in a thousand years?'

You could almost hear Canticle's brain working.

'Take your time,' said Brains. 'There's no rush.'

Canticle leaned back and closed his eyes to help him think. 'Let me see...once in a moment....no, twice in a moment....once in a minute...Hmmm!' Over and over it he went. But the answer wouldn't come. Then he had it.

'I know,' he said as he opened his eyes. 'The letter M! That occurs once in a minute. Twice in a moment. But never in a thousand years!'

But there was nobody there to hear him. Sandy, Billy, Brains, Grenville and the IDT bike had gone.

Billy was right. Canticle was a birdbrain.


Out of sight, along the road, Sandy, Billy, Brains and Grenville were sitting on the IDT bike. They were going home at last.

'Goodbye, Badlidrempt!' shouted Sandy. 'I hope we never see you again.'

'So do I!' shouted Billy.

'Me too!' yelled Brains.

'Ruff! Ruff! Ruff!' Grenville definitely agreed with that.

They started to pedal. The bike started to move. Up and down. Side to side. Round and about. And forward. Faster and faster along the road. Building up speed to the point where Brains threw the lever.

The deep rumble began. It grew louder. Then – it died away again.

There was no ear-splitting whine. No shimmering. No fading away at the edges. Nothing. The bike just kept rolling along the road.

Brains slammed on the brakes and jumped off.

'What's wrong?' said Billy.

'Is it broken?' asked Sandy.

'Uuuurrggghhh?' Grenville was as puzzled as everybody else.

'It's not broken,' said Brains. 'It just can't carry us all. We're too heavy for it.'

'But it got us all here,' said Billy.

'No,' said Sandy. 'It only brought three of us. Brains was already here.'

'So what do we do?' wailed Billy.

'We're stuck here for good,' said Brains. 'Unless I can make another bike.'

Brains slumped to the ground. He was just in time. There was a distant bang and the shot from a treble-barrelled shotgun flew over his head.

'Oh no!' moaned Sandy. 'Them again!'

They were still some distance away, but Grazzo's Hordes were coming at them from every side. Led by the evil Grazzo himself.

The second barrel exploded. It hit the ground near Billy's foot.

There was only one thing to do. Brains waved his handkerchief in the air. 'White flag!' he shouted. 'We surrender!'

But Grenville had other ideas. He jumped down off the bike and grabbed Brains by the seat of his pants. Then he dragged him over to the IDT bike.

'Woah! Woah!' he barked.

'He wants you to get on the bike,' said Billy.

'It's no good, Grenville!' shouted Brains. 'There's too many of us.'

But Grenville wasn't giving up. He kept barking until Brains climbed onto the saddle. Then he started to back away.

'What's he doing?' said Sandy. But she knew really.

Grenville kept on backing away. Then with one last bark he turned and ran off down the road.

'Grenville! Come back!' Brains screamed. But Grenville just kept on running.

Brains turned to Sandy. 'What's he doing, Sandy? Where's he going?'

There were tears rolling down Sandy's cheeks. 'Away!' she sniffed. 'Without him there's only three of us. The bike will work now.'

'But we can't go without Grenville,' Billy gulped.

'We've got to,' said Sandy, fighting back the

tears. 'It's the only way. And it's what he wanted!' She started to pedal. 'Come on,' she shouted angrily. 'Pedal! Or we'll all get caught.'

Billy and Brains pedalled.

This time when Brains threw the lever everything worked and Badlidrempt was just a blur.

The last thing they saw was Grenville. He was heading straight for Grazzo.

# Chapter 17

---

They were back. The IDT bike landed just where it had taken off. In Brains's back garden. As it came to a stop the front wheel fell off. Sandy, Brains and Billy tumbled forward onto the ground. The IDT bike had made it. But only just. The strain of the return journey through The Dimensions had almost been too much. It was only luck that had seen them safely home.

Sandy, Billy and Brains looked around. Then they jumped up and hugged each other. They were home. There had been times when they thought they would never see it again. But here they were. And the strange thing was, it was still the same day. Nobody had even noticed that they were missing.

'This is amazing,' Sandy said. 'Everything is just as we left it.'

'No, it isn't,' Brains pointed across at a pile of freshly dug earth right in the middle of the lawn. 'Who's been digging holes in the lawn?'

Billy laughed. 'Oh that was just –' Billy stopped.

'Just who?' asked Brains.

'Grenville!' said Sandy. 'He was digging for bones.'

'Grenville?'

Suddenly Brains realised the full horror of what had happened. Grenville – the craziest dog in the world. The bravest dog in the world. The best dog in the world. Grenville had been left behind. Left behind to face up to the evil Grazzo all by himself. In that crazy, terrible Land of Badlidrempt. He didn't stand a chance.

Even now he was probably locked away in some damp, gloomy cell. Eating mouldy bread and drinking smelly water. Waiting for the moment when the iron gate would open. The crowd would roar. And the Seven Headed Zaldir would lumber forward into the Circus Ring. Necks weaving from side to side. Tongues flicking out. Ready to strike. It was too awful to think about.

Sandy touched Brains. Billy turned his back. He didn't want anybody to see the wet marks on his face.

'I should never have left him behind,' said Brains quietly.

'There was nothing else we could do,' Sandy told him tearfully. 'We would all have been caught if we'd stayed. Besides, it's what Grenville wanted. He knew he was going to get caught. But he didn't care. Just as long as we got away.'

'But he was the best friend I ever had,' said Brains. 'And now he's gone.'

Suddenly Billy turned round. 'Well there's no point us crying about it, is there? Let's do something.'

'Do what?' asked Sandy.

'Go back for him, I suppose,' said Billy.

'Back? Back to Badlidrempt?'

Sandy and Brains looked at each other. They knew Billy was right. They could never be happy without Grenville.

They might not succeed. But they had to try and get him back. Even if it meant putting themselves in danger again.

'We'll need two bikes,' said Brains. 'I'll repair this one and build another. Let's get the plans.'

Sandy, Billy and Brains raced towards the shed. Billy trod on a bone that Grenville had left lying on the path. He fell headfirst into a rose bush.

Sandy and Brains pulled him out.

'That dopey dog,' snarled Billy. 'Leave him where he is.'

But Billy didn't mean it. Not really. Even if he did, he still helped build the new IDT bike.

'I've made a few improvements,' Brains announced as he climbed onto one of the bikes. 'They shouldn't be so hard to pedal now.'

Billy and Sandy climbed onto the other IDT bike.

'Ready?' asked Brains.

'Ready!' said Sandy.

'Badlidrempt here we come!' shouted Billy.

They started to pedal.

Brains was right. It was easier. Within a few seconds the sound of a travelling IDT bike was filling the air. But something was wrong. Neither Brains nor Sandy had pushed the levers on their bikes.

They stopped pedalling. The sound was still there. And it was getting louder. And louder. And louder.

'What's going on?' yelled Sandy.

'I don't know. Sounds like another IDT bike. But it can't be.'

But it could be. The next moment, an IDT bike exploded out of nowhere and crashed into the shed.

As the dust settled again, they saw them.

There. Propped up against the shed. In a mass of splintered wood and bent bike sat a very dazed and bewildered Squirm.

And next to Squirm, sat a very excited and happy –

'Grenville!' shouted Brains, Sandy and Billy.

Yes, it was Grenville. Away from Badlidrempt. Safe from the evil Grazzo. Back home where he belonged.

At first, nobody moved, then Billy, Sandy, Brains and Grenville hurled themselves together in a giant, squirming, cheering, laughing, barking heap.

After a while, they rolled apart and sat up. It was then that they remembered Squirm.

He was still sitting, propped against the shed. Staring into space. Mouth open. Hair standing on end. He looked like somebody who'd just woken from a nightmare. Not sure whether he was awake. Or if the dream was still going on.

'Squirm!' said Billy. 'The creepy, slimy, nasty, no-good Squirm! Here! On his own. At our mercy.'

Squirm's eyes came back to life. He stared at Billy, Sandy and Brains in terror.

He had good reason. They were walking

towards him. He didn't think they were going
to give him a welcoming hug. They weren't.
They were going to get their own back for all
the horrible things that had happened to them
in Badlidrempt.

But suddenly there was something in front of
them. It was Grenville. He was blocking their
way. Stopping them from getting at Squirm.

'Dopey dog!' snapped Billy. 'Shift out the way.'

But Grenville stayed put. Nobody was going
to hurt Squirm. Not while he was there.

Billy, Sandy and Brains were at a loss. What
was going on? Then Brains realised. He'd been
so happy to see Grenville that he hadn't asked
the obvious questions. How had Grenville
escaped? Where had the IDT bike come from?
And what was Squirm doing there?

There was only one possible answer. Squirm
had helped Grenville escape.

'Grenville? Did he help you get away?' Brains
asked.

Grenville's tail started to wag. 'Woah! Woah!'
he barked. Then he turned and licked Squirm's
face.

For a moment Squirm seemed to think that
Grenville was going to eat him. But then a
smile came to his face.

'The Hairy Creature,' he said. 'I think he like me now.'

The Hairy Creature did like Squirm now. And so did Brains, Sandy and Billy once they'd heard Squirm's story.

'Grazzo capture the Hairy Creature and take him back to feed to the Zaldir,' he told them. 'But I can not let him do this. The Hairy Creature was very brave. To stay behind so that his friends could escape from the Land of Badlidrempt. So in the night I let the Hairy Creature out and take him to where Grazzo has hidden the special machine.'

Grenville gave Squirm another lick.

'But the Hairy Creature cannot work the machine by himself,' Squirm continued. 'So I come with him. Now Grazzo will be after me. I think it is Squirm who will end in the belly of the Zaldir.'

Squirm looked so frightened and miserable that Sandy held his hand.

'It's all right,' she said. 'We won't send you back. Not now you've saved Grenville. Will we?'

Sandy turned to Brains and Billy.

'No,' said Brains.

'Suppose not,' said Billy. 'But why did you do it? I thought you were Grazzo's friend.'

Squirm shook his head sadly. 'Not his friend. Grazzo has no friends. Only the people who are afraid of him. That is all he wants. For much time I am frightened of Grazzo. And I try hard to be like him. But I just not nasty enough.'

'No, you're not,' said Sandy. 'And you should be glad you're not. Shouldn't he, Brains?'

But Brains didn't answer. He had that far away look in his eyes. The look that said he'd got an idea for a new invention.

'Oh no!' said Billy. 'I don't like that look at all.'

'Nor me,' groaned Sandy.

'Woah! Woah!'

Grenville didn't like it either.

'It's all right,' said Brains. 'This invention is going to be totally different from the IDT bikes. There won't be any danger at all.'

'Are you sure?' asked Sandy.

'Certain!' said Brains.

'Just as long as we don't have to go back to Badlidrempt,' said Billy.

'Ruff!' Grenville agreed.

'Oh no!' said Brains. 'We won't be going back to Badlidrempt. Not ever. Never!'

But Brains was wrong. One day they would have to go back to the Land of Badlidrempt.

Even though they didn't want to.
  But that's a different story altogether.